Sugar

Also by Kevin Semeniuk

Collections of Poetry

Love Letters
Hearts of Grace
Tales of Sorrow
In No Particular Order
Love Grace & Sorrow in No Particular Order
Revelation

Novels/Fiction

Sweeping with God
Grace in October

Sugar

Kevin Semeniuk

Fifteen for HOPE

Fifteen for HOPE Publishing

Cover design by Pencil Fingerz
Printed and bound in Canada
Second Print
Fifteen for **HOPE**
www.kevinsemeniuk.ca
Love

INTRODUCTION

For as long as I can remember dreaming was always the one place where I felt the most comfortable; most like the person I was but never had the chance to be. If I could have, I would've spent my entire childhood asleep just to be able to dream beyond the life I was in...until I met Hope.

Chapter 1

When I was just a baby, my mother left me on the front doorstep of my grandparents' house with a note pinned to my blanket that read, "*I kant do this he yurs now*". I may never had known about the note but my grandmother had it posted on the refrigerator and moved it up with each inch that I grew so that my eyes were always in view of it. I guess it was her way of reminding me of the burden that I brought upon her life.

My grandmother was very stern in her speech, when she chose to speak, but as far as rules or demands went she was fine so long as my time spent around her or within her tiny house was minimal. My grandfather died nearly a year after I was left with them so I didn't get to know him at all; at least not that I remember. Our neighbor would tell me stories, as I grew in years, how in love my grandparents were and how after my grandfather died my grand- mother just wasn't ever the same. They were always adamant, when telling me their stories, to let me know that she wasn't *always* a reflection of her current state. I never held anything against her anyway, I wasn't her child and she was stuck with me. The way I saw it was, *at least she kept me*, unlike my own mother.

I spent a lot of time with the neighbors, especially the lady of the house, Ms. Violet. I was never enrolled in school so Ms. Violet would spend time with me, teaching me basic writing skills along with some mathematics and odd bits of history. I think most of the history was taught *off the cuff* though because "by the hand of God himself" found its way into almost every lesson or story she referred to. I didn't mind nor did I ever question her lessons, I was always just happy to be there.

Ms. Violet was the kindest woman I'd ever met. Now granted, I'd never spent much time around too many other people but she was sure good to me. Her and my grandparents had been neighbors since *"the dawn of time"* as she put it, and she always did everything that she could to nurture me. She taught me manners, showed me how cook a little bit and to wash and dry dishes and even how to scrub stains out of my clothes with a rock and a board. She told me that as long as she had breath in her "old lungs", she'd do all that she could to make sure I went out into the world with everything I needed to be a man of respect, and a gentleman, as she would say. I followed her around like a lost puppy whenever she would have me, which was far more often than not.

Her husband's name was Mr. Charlie; he was just as kind as Ms. Violet only he wasn't at home as much so his and my time spent together wasn't as frequent. He did teach me a few things though, like how to snare a rabbit and swing an axe. We'd gone fishing quite a few times as well but I didn't know how to swim, which always kept me pretty close to the waters' edge, and I'd always had a fear of the water; anything outside of a bathtub or shallow puddle anyway.

Mr. Charlie worked at the lumber mill just a few miles away, which worked out well for him because they didn't have a vehicle, like most folks where we lived, so he would walk every day to and from the mill. Each day he came home to Ms. Violet with a fresh bundle of wild flowers that he'd pick on his walk home. If ever I was around when he got home he'd hold out the flowers for me to pick one or two out and encourage me to take them home to my grand-mother. I assured him that she didn't have any interest in flowers but he always softly said the same thing, "she'll like 'em, son, trus' me...every woman likes flowers", then he'd send me on my way. My grandmother could never be bothered with them, just like I said, and she'd toss them out the second I gave them to her, depending on how close to the trashcan she was. I still always gathered them back up or picked them out of the trash and I'd set them in an old can filled with water on the window sill over the kitchen sink. She never bothered with them after that and I'd replace them with fresh one's every time Mr. Charlie sent me home with some; it was our own little ritual. I think sometimes she fought harder to be miserable than she really was.

CHAPTER 2

One spring, my grandmother and I were out back planting the garden when a car pulled up the driveway, which was really more of just a beaten path from the odd visitor, and was shared between my grandmother and Ms. Violet and Mr. Charlie's house. Normally I wouldn't have paid much attention to such a thing but the driver was honking the horn so rapidly I couldn't help but watch to see what all the fuss was about. As my grandmother shouted at me to keep seeding and to watch my step as I stumbled across the freshly planted rows, I watched curiously while Ms. Violet walked sideways down her front steps toward the car. She approached the passenger door and opened it to see inside. I could hear yelling from inside the car, then a woman stepped out from the drivers' side and opened up the trunk. She pulled out a few pieces of luggage and threw them on the grass then went around to the back door, opened it, and assisted a young girl from the backseat out and onto the driveway. As the girl stepped out Ms. Violet cupped the girls' face in her hands and smothered her with kisses. The woman continued to rant, shouting and waving her hands in the air, although I still couldn't make out what she was saying, until she got back in the car and drove off across my grandmothers' front lawn.

I stood still, watching, as Ms. Violet blanketed the young girl in her arms, guiding her around to the back of the house and then inside. Ms. Violet made a trip back outside by herself to grab the luggage off the front lawn, and without so much as looking at me or my grandmother, she gathered the few items and went back inside.

"Hey, grandma...who's that?" I asked curiously.

"Who's **who**?" she snipped back.

"That girl...that girl who jus got let off at Ms. Violets', jus now," I explained as I stared across the yard.

"I dunno, and that ain't none 'uh my business…just like it ain't none 'uh yours. We got work to do here, work that I'd like to finish before the sun falls," she replied sharply.

"Yes ma'am," I answered softly, knowing her tone.

One thing I never formed a habit of was disobeying or arguing with my grandmother. She was easy to live around for the most part but when she said *enough*, it was enough. I never pushed her past that and I knew it in her tone, it didn't take much.

Every few minutes as we continued to seed the soil with hopeful new life I would look up to check on Ms. Violets' house, curiously, waiting to see someone come outside, but no one did.

My grandmother went into the house shortly before me to fix supper, leaving me to finish up in the garden.

I was hoping Ms. Violet would stick her head outside and call me over to introduce me to her young visitor but she never did. The curiosity and anticipation was killing me. I never thought of myself as a nosey child but I didn't have any friends and surely never had any visitors of my own, so I was making it my business to find out who this one was.

Once I was finished up in the garden my grandmother called me in for supper.

We sat across from each other, as we always did, not saying much of anything to one another. My mind was next door at Ms. Violet's house anyway, picturing what was going on in there as I thought of a reason to go visit after dinner.

"Slow-down, boy, you gonna choke…and I ain't about to give you no smack on the back when you do," my grandmother belted.

"Yes, ma'am," I answered softly.

I finished eating as quick as I could and then washed and dried dishes while my grandmother sat at the table filling her old tobacco can with fresh ashes, smoking a cigarette.

"Okay, grandma, I'm gonna go outside for a bit...I'm all done," I chirped.

"Go on then," she replied.

"Thanks for supper," I said as I went out the back door from the kitchen.

"Enough with the racket, jus get," she barked.

Just as I stepped out back I could hear Mr. Charlie walking up to the house. You could never mistake his footsteps dragging across the scattered bits of gravel, as he was such a large man.

As I heard him near I followed up behind him hoping to get an invite inside to meet their guest.

"Evenin', Mr. Charlie," I chirped as I crept up behind him.

"Poor Boy...why you almost scared me straight outta my pants, son...I didn't even hear you comin'," he exclaimed.

"Just finished dinner, sir, didn't mean to startle you," I explained, happy to see him.

"No need to be sorry, son, I'm old is all and it don't take much to gimme a stir," he said, laughing lightly at himself as he patted me on the head.

"Nah, I seen old, sir, seen it in church...and you ain't it," I said playfully.

"I'm too old...too old to remember and too tired to try," he chuckled.

"You comin' in or you just gonna stand there?" he asked of me as I stood waiting for an invite.

I followed his lead and stepped in behind him into the back porch of their home.

As I waited while he hung his jacket I could hear light laughter from the kitchen just on the other side of the door. There were two voices, one familiar and one I hadn't heard before; a young voice, a girl.

"Soundin' like we got some company," Mr. Charlie mumbled as he opened the door leaving the porch.

I was busy trying to see around his large frame to get a first glance at the stranger I had been thinking about all day, but I was out of luck.

Mr. Charlie and Ms. Violet greeted each other, as they always did, with a kiss on the cheek and a few playful words as he handed her a small bundle of freshly picked wild flowers from his walk home. I sat down at the kitchen table and watched her mix something in a bowl as she stood beside the stove where she had supper cooking. There wasn't a lot of room in the house, much like my grand-mothers', so my curiosity was growing in anticipation for the young voice to come out from hiding.

"Were my old ears playing tricks on me or did I hear another voice when I was hangin' my coat?" Mr. Charlie asked of his wife.

"There she is! Baby, you had your grandfather thinking he was losin' his poor mind," Ms. Violet spoke with a great joy.

I turned as I sat in my chair to get a look at the cause of my curiosity. Before she could open her mouth to say anything Mr. Charlie had her wrapped so tight against him in a hug that she was sure to be losing her breath.

I remember the feeling I had as I smiled, watching his expression of love; the entire house lit up, I'm sure of it. I believe that was my first experience witnessing such an honest, and very proud, sharing of love.

It began to make me feel uneasy so I turned back to face the table as they hugged and stayed in their moment for a few minutes, while Mr. Charlie softly spoke to her.

Ms. Violet walked over toward me and rested her hand over mine as I sat quietly at the table. She smiled at me, surely able to sense my sudden feelings of unease, then simply whispered, *"it's okay child"*.

Until that moment I hadn't ever seen such a pure display of love. Often I would see Mr. Charlie and Ms. Violet being playful and loving with each other and I always knew it was love, but from an adult toward a child, I'd never had a chance to witness before that moment. At first it was quite warming to watch but as I slowly realized that it was something I'd never experienced, it suddenly made me uncomfortable. Even for my age, I very clearly remember the change in thought and then Ms. Violet comforting me, picking up on my emotion.

"Sugar, I want you to meet someone, someone real special, our young neighbor, our friend...this here is, Poor Boy," Ms. Violet spoke up as the two parted from their hug.

"Why they call you Poor Boy?" the girl asked as she turned out from Mr. Charlie's grip.

"'Cause it's my name," I answered with certainty.

I could feel my face turn red; she was so pretty.

My grandmother, for as cranky and sometimes seemingly miserable as she could be, always wore this one particular perfume. It sat on her chest of drawers in her bedroom next to a picture of my grandfather. I often wondered why she still wore it, because of the obvious contrast between its scent and her, or if maybe she was just wearing it for him; if that was something that he loved about her, her scent, and that was how she kept him near. No matter how she ever treated me, her perfume made her more real; it helped me make some sense of her.

In an instant, that's how this young girl made me feel, like things just made sense.

"Go on, Sugar, introduce yourself," Mr. Charlie spoke up.

"I'm 'uh, I'm Hope," she said softly as she reached out to shake my hand.

I stood to my feet and shook her hand as I smiled, not taking my eyes off of her.

"Now, Sugar's gonna be staying with us for a while, so you two will be seeing a lot of each other, no doubt," Ms. Violet explained as she smiled from ear to ear.

I smiled at Hope until she looked away, shyly, nestling her face against Mr. Charlie's side.

"You be joinin' us for dinner, Poor Boy?" Ms. Violet asked.

"Please, ma'am, if it ain't no worry," I replied, smiling.

I was still full from the meal I shared with my grandmother, no more than one hour before, but I didn't want to pass up a moment to be near Hope. I was immediately drawn to her and the new love that filled the air with her arrival.

"You know there's always a place for you at our table, child," she said, smiling, as she patted me on the head.

"Yes, ma'am, thank you," I answered, smiling at Hope.

The four of us sat down for dinner, passing around each others' plate while Ms. Violet loaded them up. The small talk consisted mostly of Ms. Violet and Mr. Charlie speaking about his day at work and them making plans to put their garden in, as they had noticed my grandmother's being planted. As they talked about how many rows of what vegetables they were going to plant this year, Hope and I were becoming acquainted with each other through silence and shy smiles.

Their house wasn't all that much bigger than my grandmothers' but it did have one extra bedroom which was now, by the looks of it, going to be occupied by Hope.

Once our plates were cleared and I was stuffed like an expensive pillow, Mr. Charlie and I cleaned up and did the dishes; he washed and I dried. Hope and Ms. Violet sat at the table just a few feet away from us, talking softly amongst themselves. I could only hear bits and pieces over the clanging of dishes in the sink and Mr. Charlie talking to me. Ms. Violet was consoling Hope, letting her know that she was safe now and that she had nothing to worry about. I was curious to know all about her; where she came from, who she belonged to and why she was now here. In time, I told myself, all my questions and wonders would be answered.

Shortly after we finished up with the dishes it was time for me to go home; we all said goodbye to each other and I left out the back porch.

The sun was ducking down behind the trees and as I neared the house I could smell cigarette smoke wafting from the backyard.

"Jus what exactly do ya'll get into over there anyway?" my grand-mother asked as I got close enough to see her sitting out back.

"Hi, grandma," I said as I waved to her.

"That ain't no answer...you all 'uh sudden hard 'uh hearing?" she muttered.

"No, ma'am...we was jus visiting, that's all, same as always," I answered calmly.

"Oh, well look at you, ain't you clever?" she said with her cigarette hanging out one side of her mouth.

"No ma'am," I insisted softly as I opened the door and went into the house.

I washed up in the sink, got changed and grabbed my blankets to make my bed on the sofa.

By the time I tucked myself into bed my grandmother had come back in the house and went off to her bedroom.

"G'night, grandma," I shouted, as I always did before bed.

She didn't reply. She never did but it gave me comfort to say it anyway; it kept me from feeling alone in the house on that old sofa.

I fell asleep smiling about my new neighbor and hopeful soon to be friend.

CHAPTER 3

The next morning, I was up, had my blankets all folded and put away and had breakfast made for my grandmother before she woke up. I often cooked breakfast for her, mostly when I was able to wake up before her though, so I didn't have her in my ear the whole time telling me that I was doing it all wrong or nudging me out of the way to do it herself.

Mr. Charlie taught me how to cook breakfast. He said that every woman deserved to have their day begin and end with being appreciated, so that everything that *they* did in between they would know mattered. So every morning, no matter what, he would cook for Ms. Violet, and every evening after dinner he would do the dishes. That's how he showed his appreciation for her; well that, and his picking fresh flowers for her, even if just one, he would tear it from the ground and deliver it to his wife. It wasn't as though he worshipped her or did anything that seemed like it was forced; he just did what he could to make sure his love and admiration for her was always shown, that it was always present. His gestures were very natural and smooth, just as though there wasn't any other way to treat a woman; and her response was the same. It was always a very calming atmosphere to be in, from the first time I was present to witness it, it was just very easy to be around.

I left my grandmothers' breakfast covered and set at the table as I heard her making her way out of bed in the next room, and then I went next door.

Just as I knocked on the back porch, Mr. Charlie was heading out with his lunch pail in hand, on his way down to the mill.

"Mornin', Poor Boy; another beautiful mornin'…I see the good lord ain't forgot about us jus yet. The girls are up, they jus finishin' they breakfast," he said with a chirp as he held open the door for me to go in under his arm.

"Thank you, sir, you have a good day at work," I replied as I scurried into the house.

"Good mornin' ma'am, mornin' Hope," I said cheerfully as I stepped into the kitchen from the back porch.

"Good mornin' to you too, darlin'…you hungry?" Ms. Violet spoke with a spark in her voice as she sat beside Hope at the table, eating.

"Nah, I'm okay, thank you, ma'am, but I jus had my breakfast," I answered, looking over at Hope as she looked shyly back at me.

I sat down at the table to visit with Ms. Violet as her and Hope, who didn't say much, finished eating. Once they were done, I started cleaning up their dishes and took them to wash in the sink.

"That's okay, child, you ain't got to clean up, I got others to do there too," Ms. Violet spoke up.

"It's okay, ma'am, jus pass 'em off to me 'n I can do them ones too," I answered, proud to be of some help.

"Them ones?" she questioned sternly.

"Those ones, ma'am," I replied, smiling.

Ms. Violet always did her best to catch me using poor English when I spoke; or *"a lazy mans' English"* as she called it. And when she did she'd be sure to have me correct myself or she'd talk me through it if I just didn't know any better. She explained to me that I should *learn* to know better, and strive to be better but more importantly I should *want* to be better. She said that I shouldn't always listen to how she's saying something but rather to *what* she was saying. In that, she said, it would teach me how to speak like a gentleman.

I caught Hope smiling, still sitting at the kitchen table, at my misfortune of having an English lesson first thing in the morning. I smiled back, happy to be the cause for her brief moment of subtle delight.

"Sugar, you wanna give Poor Boy a hand with the dishes?" Ms. Violet asked of Hope.

"Yes ma'am," Hope answered as she stood up to come help me.

As I waited for Hope to join me at my side, I heard a light squeaking upon her footsteps.

I hadn't paid attention to her walk in our previous encounter so I was slightly taken back when I first watched her come toward me.

Beneath her green, knee high dress, I caught the bottom half of what appeared to be some sort of leg brace. It looked to be metal, and definitely sounded rusty, with what looked like hinges on either side of her knee. She walked with a slight hop, favoring her braced leg. I'd never seen such a thing in my short and quite sheltered life but other than the initial wonder or slight surprise, it didn't faze me for more than the time it took her to reach my side at the sink.

She looked at me with blushed cheeks as she appeared to be embarrassed with me staring at her so I smiled and splashed water at her, playfully, to throw off the moment. She laughed and took a stand next to me as she wiped the drops of soapy water from her face.

Ms. Violet shook her head, smiling, as she began to hum; which was something that she did almost more than she would speak.

The three of us played around as we finished washing and drying the dishes, while Ms. Violet hummed her way through stacking them in their dedicated space behind the doors of her cupboards.

While Ms. Violet began to prepare lunch and then supper for when Mr. Charlie got home, along with her daily routine of baking, she scooted Hope and I outside to play. She warned Hope to go easy and not do anything too uncomfortable but Hope didn't seem very concerned.

Neither of us had much of anything to mess around with, as far as toys went, so we spent most of our time talking; each of us trying to figure out as much as we could about the other.

"Why they call you Poor Boy?" she questioned me.

"It's uh, it's kinda stupid...." I started, nervously, shaking my head.

"That's okay, I think we all got a little stupid in our lives," she said as she squinted against the sun.

"Well, my mother, she dropped me off on my grandmothers' doorstep when I was jus a baby. I guess she couldn't take it no more...bein' a mom, so she left me; left me for my grandmother to try 'n do right. Me, I wasn't given no name, not since I could listen has anyone called me anythin' but Poor Boy. I ain't dumb though, I know they call me that 'cause I was left without a care by my own mother, but it don't make no difference to me, it's all I know. I ain't never had no birthday and I ain't got no real name," I explained; and for the first time in my life I was hearing it out loud.

"Wait...you ain't never had no birthday...ever?" she asked, sounding surprised.

"Nope...no one knows when I was born. My momma's the only one who know that, and she ain't never looked back after leavin' me here," I replied simply.

"So jus how old are you then?" she questioned curiously.

"Don't know. I asked Ms. Violet once if she had a clue but she didn't even know my grandmother had me until my grandfather passed," I answered, tiring of the subject.

"How old are you?" I asked.

"Don't know," she answered softly, hiding her mouth with her hands.

"You jus foolin' with me now, 'cause 'uh what I said," I accused her, playfully.

"I ain't...honest as the sun, I ain't," she insisted, standing up straight.

"How's that, how can you not know?" I asked, surprised.

"I never had nobody to tell me, same as you," she answered, looking me straight in the eyes.

"You don't got no parents neither?" I questioned, squinting.

"Nope, not since I was jus little. My daddy, he died, and then my momma left me with my aunty...and that's who dropped me here. I ain't never seen my grandparents since I was jus a baby neither," she explained.

"When's your aunty coming back to get you?" I asked curiously.

"Don't think she is; she told my grandma that she done with me, said she ain't fussin' over me no more and that I was too big 'uh pain in her big 'ol behind," she said, with a very calm tone.

"She said that?" I belted out.

"Well, not the part about her havin' a big behind, but...yeah," she replied.

I couldn't believe how much her story and mine were alike.

Up until that point in time I hadn't come across too many other kids, other than at church, and I didn't have any friends, so to find one right next door who was as pretty as she was and so much like me...something came alive inside me in that moment.

We continued to walk and stop briefly every few minutes so she could rest her leg, talking about whatever came to mind; mostly getting to know each other and what our interests were and such.

I stayed to her right side, which was downwind from her, as we walked, and I couldn't stop sticking my nose out to smell the air; the breeze was dusting me with her perfume. My mind kept going blank and I was getting lost in what we were talking about. I think for a moment she might have thought I was dimwitted because I kept repeating, *"uhhh, what was I saying?"* - but the simple truth is that I felt like I was just learning how to speak because of whatever it was that she had sprayed on herself that morning.

The day was well on its way as the sun was growing in strength.

Throughout my years without any friends I had done a lot of exploring on my own in the backwoods just behind my grandmothers' house.

I led Hope into the woods to one of my discovered places of solo refuge.

Slowly, we made our way as I helped her climb over some big, old, fallen trees covered in years of moss and stories of my visits. We found ourselves deep in the shadows of history beneath the rooftop of trees. I acted as a tour guide, speaking quite proper as I repeated events that I had once made up for my own enjoyment while I was exploring the woods alone.

"This is where they first came to witness the full power of the King and his army," I spoke with excitement.

"Huh?" she asked, confused.

"Ssshhh, they comin'...duck!" I whispered playfully as I pulled on her arm to duck down behind a pile of dead trees.

"You crazy...I don't see no one," she stated, standing still at my side.

"False alarm...that was a close call," I said as I stood to my feet.

Hope smiled at me with a look of uncertainty.

"You okay?" she questioned, curiously.

"Me? Of course I'm okay. You okay?" I asked, teasing her.

"I'm fine...I'm jus fine," she answered, still smiling.

We wandered around for a while as I continued the tour, still helping her get over obstructions, until we could hear the faint shouting of Ms. Violet calling us for lunch, and then we took a shortcut I knew back toward the house.

"C'mon children, hurry up now!" Ms. Violet shouted from the back porch as we neared.

"We coming, ma'am," I spoke on our behalf.

Hope appeared to be really favoring her braced leg. She was walking quite light on it, making her hop a bit more noticeable than when we'd first set out.

"You okay?" I asked as I looked down at her leg.

"I'm fine," she answered sternly.

"Where'd ya'll disappear to so fast?" Ms. Violet asked as we entered the house.

"We was jus back in the woods; I was showin' Hope around, givin' her the tour," I answered, full of fresh air.

"Sugar, you okay, your leg givin' you some grief?" she asked of Hope.

"Jus like I told him...*I'm fine*," Hope answered, again quite stern.

"Tough as a mule is stubborn, this one is; she get that from her daddy, rest in peace," Ms. Violet said as she gently patted Hope on the top of her head.

"That your son, her daddy?" I asked Ms. Violet.

"Sure is, and a fine young man he was but, well, he's with God now," she said with a smile as she scurried around her undersized kitchen, setting lunch.

Hope didn't say much, she just sat quietly waiting to begin eating.

On the table set in front of each of us was a bowl of freshly made hot soup and warm buns straight from the oven. It didn't matter that the temperature outside was rapidly climbing to a degree hot enough to fry an egg on a rock, hot soup is what was for lunch and we all sat, sweating, spooning it into our mouths. Ms. Violet kept a small cloth loose in one hand, which she used in between bites to wipe the sweat from her brow, while Hope and I, for the most part, let our sweat fall from the tips of our noses and chins onto the table below. Few words were ever spoken during meals under such conditions; it was get in, eat and get out.

After lunch, Ms. Violet, out of concern, ordered Hope to stay within view of the house and to take it easy on her leg. She didn't want her running around or doing anything too strenuous which might cause her to get hurt. Hope wasn't too happy about being coddled and insisted that she was fine but Ms. Violet was quite adamant about her decision.

Hope and I sat visiting in the shade under a tree by the garden. She expressed her distaste for feeling pitied over the condition of her leg. I found it quite easy to be near her, even with her frustration toward attention, she was quickly becoming my first real friend.

As the sun was nearing its peak we were losing our shade so we moved over to my yard to lean against my grandmothers' small wooden shed. I was tearing handfuls of grass from the ground and blowing them, with all of my might, into Hopes' hair.

"Hey grandma!" I shouted as my grandmother came out toward the garden from the house.

As water spilled out from the watering can that she carried to sprinkle over her tomato plants, she looked over at us then looked straight away, back on the path to her plants.

"Grandma, this is Hope...my friend from next door; she Ms. Violet's granddaughter," I yelled, looking for a response.

*"Am I blind, child?...*I can see her," she replied, leaning to one side with her opposite arm held out to help balance carrying the watering can.

"Good afternoon, ma'am, you need some help?" Hope spoke up.

"I'm fine," my grandmother snarled.

Hope looked over at me, smiled and shrugged her shoulders; I did the same in return.

We sat quietly, whispering mostly, as we watched my grandmother water her tomato plants, but she didn't so much as even look over in our direction. With a cigarette hanging out of her mouth and the watering can in her hand, she went back into the house leaving the can by the back door.

"She always that way?" Hope asked of my grandmother.

"Pretty much," I answered simply, nodding my head as I looked toward the house.

I was so used to my grandmother acting and reacting just one way to me for so many years that it really didn't even register anymore, but having someone else notice it made me a little frustrated; that was new.

That evening, Hope and I went our separate ways for supper. My grandmother would've been more than happy not to feed me but had she prepared me a plate and I failed to show up for supper, I surely would've been eating it cold for breakfast.

"You done messin' around with that girl now?" my grandmother asked as I sat down for supper.

"We wasn't messin' around grandma, we was jus playing, getting to know each other...and somehow, we a lot alike," I answered with a chirp.

"You was messin' around, I saw yah doin' so...and if I catch you rippin' my grass outta the ground again to blow in that girls' face, you gonna be sorry. You hear me?" she snapped at me.

"Yes ma'am," I answered simply.

I couldn't wait to get away from the table to go back next door and visit.

As fast as I could, without angering my grandmother, I shoveled down my supper, cleaned up and took off out the back door.

I spent the evening next door sitting around the kitchen table, laughing and visiting with Hope and both Mr. Charlie and Ms. Violet. We had some fresh warm pie and vanilla ice cream as we sat and listened to one of Mr. Charlie's stories.

He always had a way with words when he would tell a story; so magical and full of wonder. He created such an escape with the way he would explain colors and the characters, it was as though you were watching it unfold right in front of your eyes. This story in particular was one I hadn't heard before, which he claimed was in fact true. It was about a young boy and girl, he said near the ages of Hope and me, who had discovered a magical land in a forest while they were out exploring one day. He said that they were orphans and had drifted from home to home but could never find one that would keep them, as he put it, so they just set out on their own. With nothing more than the clothes on their backs and some food they had managed to scrounge up they came across a magical door that lead into a land outside of this world, in the forest they had found refuge in, covered in vines and hidden to the eye of even the best marksmen, at the foot of a tree that stretched high up into the heavens.

He went on talking as we held on to every word, savoring each one as though it was the last he would set free and the more he would unveil the more I began to believe in what he was saying. I was gone, beyond the words, I had disappeared from the room.

After the better part of the evening had past, Mr. Charlie finished the story with, *"And that all happened right back there…back there in that very bush!"* he insisted, pointing out the kitchen window toward the very same forest which I had spent many hours exploring by myself.

"No way, that ain't true, Ms. Violet, is it…is he tellin' the truth?" I asked as I turned to look at Ms. Violet in sudden disbelief but absolute wonder.

"I think if he say so it mus be jus that…it mus be jus like he tellin' you," she happily answered with a smile.

Hope and I sat smiling, staring at each other trying to figure out if we were being fooled.

When I left late that evening I stood still under the glowing moon-light, staring up at the sky; then as a bright, shooting star danced clear across the sky I didn't skip a beat, fresh from the voice of my heart, I wished upon it with every ounce of my being.

"I wouldn't count on it," the voice of my grandmother grumbled.

She was outside, sitting in her chair at the back door, having a cigarette.

I went inside without saying anything.

As I laid on that old couch under my blankets that night, waiting to drift off to sleep, all that I could think about was Mr. Charlie's story and that forest, which might as well have been right in my own back yard, for as close as it was. What if it was true, what if that place did exist? My mind wandered throughout the night in great wonder about all of the possibilities.

Chapter 4

The next morning, after breakfast, I was waiting outside for my grandmother to walk to church with, when out from next door came Mr. Charlie, Ms. Violet and Hope; they were all dressed up and headed to church as well.

Our church was just up the road from where we lived, and every Sunday all the folks from the same stretch of road would be out walking the very same path as we did to go sing with God in an old worn down, shoulder to shoulder, sweatshop of a building. The tired white paint was peeling away from the shell of the church and the roof leaked when it rained, or sprinkled, or even when it collected dew from a humid night before, and it would drip into scattered cans placed with precise care around the floor, as well as onto the brims of the big hats that most of the women wore to match their *Sunday best*. Most of the women were busy waving small paper fans back and forth in front of their faces as they sang, while the majority of the men had a small child wrapped around their neck as they too did their best to hold a tune. That was, in the whole of my short life, the only time I was ever around people other than my grandmother, Ms. Violet or Mr. Charlie. I always stood next to my grandmother in church because I loved to hear her sing; it was like she was speaking directly to God when she sang, but then also singing because of something that she just needed to let out. Just for that small period of time, every Sunday, she would release her spirit into that old building and she would allow herself to be free.

My grandmother kept her acknowledgement of our neighbors quite short, as she had grown accustomed to doing, and I managed to lag behind in order to walk alongside Hope.

"You look nice," I said to Hope as we slowed our walk to be alone.

"I don't care much for church but I wasn't given no choice neither," she replied.

"You was so, Sugar, you was told that you could come to church or you could stay home and work the garden," Ms. Violet spoke up, giggling.

"I don't mind it, it's kinda nice actually…to hear all the singin'. You sing?" I asked, smiling at her as I walked with my hands in my pockets.

"Not to be heard, no," she answered, looking at me like I was crazy.

As we continued to walk the gathering of people grew as they left their homes, heading out to a shared destination.

Hope's demeanor began to change with every passing minute and added person joining the march. She started to become more shy and quiet, tending to hide in between myself and Mr. Charlie. I could tell that she was putting a lot of added effort into walking "normal", trying to disguise her limp. I didn't want to bring any extra attention to what she was doing so I helped her hide, in-directly, as I continued to prod her with questions and playful banter in an effort to distract her from herself.

I felt bad that she was hiding, so in that moment I made a promise to myself; I would never allow anyone to make her feel ashamed of herself, not for anything.

As we got to church, Hope stayed nestled in alongside Mr. Charlie as they found their seat upon one of the old ragged pews closer to the back, and I went up front to join my grandmother where she had gone to sit.

When I reached my grandmothers' side she looked down over her glasses at me and smiled then sat down with her hand bag, filled with tissues and peppermints, across her lap, tucked beneath the fingers of both hands. I sat down next to her, quite tight to her side as I often did, regardless of the impending heat, because at the front of the church where we were seated, was where most of the older women sat and I always ended up getting squished or even sat on for a brief moment. I had learned, depending on which woman was next to me, how to avoid getting smothered to the point of me yelping and then getting a sharp pinch in return from my grandmother for doing so. She always knew the exact spot to grab and pinch too, right inside the back of my arm. There was very rarely an escape from my grandmother when she was irritated by me.

Throughout church service I kept looking back to check on Hope and I used the very best of my hearing to try and catch even just one note of her singing but she was doing quite a good job at keeping her lips sealed. So I'd just send her a smile and quick wave then turn back around and join in the clapping and singing as I was getting nudged from side to side by the overly zealous woman next to me who was trying to find her own rhythm between waving her fan, clapping her hands, her side to side shimmy, and trying to keep in harmony with everyone else. My grandmother however, without any intention, would often over power most of the women with her voice; it would always make me shine inside to hear that kind of beauty exude from her being.

Service had come to an end and I was looking forward to the walk back home alongside Hope, but by the time I forced my way through the lingering crowd and got outside they were already gone and out of sight. My grandmother and I then made our way home, silently, side by side on the narrow gravel road.

Over the years my grandmother had grown increasingly impatient and in a hurry to make her way home after being away for even just a short time. There was a time when she would be one of the last to leave the building and I would be waiting on her every word in order to go. Or she'd go over to a friends' house afterward for tea and to play cards, dragging me along with her; but those days had grown quite distant. Now, she went to church, set her love free to God, and she quickly went back home to be alone. Even with me around she was still very much alone, and that seemed to be just how she wanted it.

After arriving back at home I changed clothes and went calling on
Hope next door.

"Why'd you leave in such a hurry?" I asked of Hope as she was
sitting outside her house on the back steps as I approached.

"Why not?" she answered, seeming irritated.

"You okay?" I asked, squinting with the sun against my face, sensing
she was unhappy.

"I'm fine," Hope said quickly in return, still yet to look up at me.

She was sitting down, hunched over her knees, dragging a twig
through the dirt around in circles. Her dress covered most of her
legs but she still pulled on it down toward her feet with her free
hand in an effort to hide the brace. It wasn't something that I cared
to bring any extra attention to so I didn't bother questioning her
any further. I could see that she went through moments of in-
security about it, from our walk to church, so I did my best to get
her mind off it.

"Wanna go play in the forest?" I asked, cheerfully.

"Not really," she replied simply.

"C'mon let's go, I jus wanna try and find something," I prodded.

"Find what?" she asked.

"Well, let's go and see," I said as I dragged my foot through the
circle she was tracing in the dirt.

"Heeyyy, what'd you do that for?" she shouted in question.

"C'mon, don't worry 'bout that, let's go...*c'mon get'up!*" I demanded
with enthusiasm.

"I don't feel like goin' no place right now," she said in return.

I stood over her, in silence, as she had begun another circle around her feet in the dirt with her twig, which was starting to wear down, as she was pressing firmly against the ground.

"You jus gonna stand there all day?" she asked of me.

"Not all day, no," I answered, breaking my silence.

I turned and walked away, heading toward the forest. I looked back, just once, and Hope didn't so much as lift her head to see me off. She kept her head buried down over her knees as she dug a small trench around her feet in the softening earth.

As I stepped through the tall grass leading into the forest I took one last look back for Hope but she wasn't anywhere in sight, so I just figured she went inside the house. I carried on into the woods, leaping and crawling onto and over anything I could manage.

Generally, when it would rain during the spring and summer it did so mostly during the night and the odd time during the day, so most of the time the forest bed would stay wet or damp until late day. The trees were all very tall and had lush green moss climbing up their trunks and any deadfall was covered in it just the same. It really was a beautiful and magical place to spend time getting lost.

Continuing on my journey of imagination I thought about the story Mr. Charlie had told to us about the hidden door somewhere in the very same forest where I now stood. Obviously my next thoughts were to seek out, and hoping to be without fail, that very door. I carefully snapped a branch, which appeared to look like a sword, off a dead tree that was lying on the ground and I began my search. Tapping and poking my stick against the trunk of almost every tree, I made my way, one by one, through what appeared to be a very strategic placing of trees. There were very few small or inferior sized trees among the giants that towered above me, so the spacing between the large trunks at ground level was quite large at some points. If it weren't for so much seasoned deadfall, it would look as though you could build a small community among the wooded bed.

"What 'chu doin'?" a familiar voice questioned slowly from behind me.

"Where'd you come from?" I returned as I could see it was Hope.

"This what you been doin' in here the whole time?" she asked, looking at me sideways.

"The whole time?" I returned. "I thought you didn't wanna come?" I prodded, smiling.

"Yeah, well," she shot back.

"Why you so mad?" I asked as I stabbed my stick into the earth.

"One 'uh them dumb boys threw mud at me when we was outside, after church...callin' me names," she stated, sounding disheartened.

"What boy, who, you know who done it?" I demanded in question.

"Name was, Nicky...I think, I think that's what they was callin' him," she answered.

"Who called him, who all was there?" I asked, feeling frustrated.

"His friends...they was all standin' around, laughin' at me, sayin' I look like a freak," she explained as she began to cry.

"Where was Mr. Charlie and Ms. Violet?" I asked softly.

"They was off talkin' to they friend," she replied, crying, rubbing the tears from her face.

"That boy, Nicky...he missin' a front tooth?" I asked curiously, trying to place a face to the boy.

"Yeah, think so...yeah, that's him," she answered as her crying slowed.

Right then, we could hear Ms. Violet calling for us to come in and have lunch.

"You wanna come back out here later?" I asked of her.

"Okay," she answered simply, wiping the last of her tears from her face.

When we reached the house, as the day was quickly heating up, Ms. Violet was waiting outside to cool off from the heat of her kitchen where she'd been cooking.

"You gonna be joinin' us, sweetheart?" she asked of me, smiling, as she fanned herself with her hand.

"Not today, ma'am, but thank you," I answered, looking over at Hope.

"Meet back here?" Hope asked, approaching the house.

"Yep, back here," I replied in short.

Hope and Ms. Violet went into the house as I went off in the direction of my own home, next door.

Instead of going home, I took off up the road toward the church; I wasn't exactly sure where to look but I was determined to find him, with or without his friends. As I approached the church I walked around it, only to find the grounds empty. I stopped to think of where I should search next just as I heard a number of loud voices and laughter from the ravine, down in behind the cemetery.

The cemetery had an old beat up fence around the outskirts of the grounds and there was a gate leading down to the ravine where they used to bury people who had *"committed crimes against their fellow man or neighbor"*, as it was often explained in stories. I hadn't ever gone exploring down that way due to a young fear that came along with the images of what it may look like, but this time I was going without hesitation.

As I stood at the gate there wasn't a clear line of sight down toward the sound of where the voices were coming from so I lifted the gate on its single warped hinge, left it open, and proceeded down. There were scattered, and mostly broken, headstones covered in vines and tall grass all along an old beaten path down the side of the ravine. The hillside was clear of any trees, but was covered in years of fallen leaves from those closest in distance. It had an eerie but kind of curious beauty about it all.

As I neared their sounds of laughter I ducked down to have a better look.

There they were, Nicky and his two friends. I knew who he was only from church, and his name from his mother as she was quite often scolding him for something during service.

He and his friends had a dog tied up to a tree with an old torn up piece of rope and they were taunting and teasing it while they whipped it with branches. The dog didn't appear to have much fight left in it as it could barely muster up a growl or even a faint bark. It looked to be quite broken, in spirit, but not visibly bleeding or horribly injured.

"Stop that!" I demanded as I stepped into visibility of the three bullies.

"What 'chu gonna do about it, *fatty*?" Nicky asked as he turned to me with his stick in hand.

His two friends swatted the dog one more time each and then turned to circle me while Nicky walked toward me. I looked at my feet and scanned the ground around them for a branch or stick of my own, to even things up, but here was nothing but grass and leaves.

"You the one who threw mud at Hope?" I asked of Nicky.

"Threw mud at who?" he snarled back.

"Hope, my friend, Hope, after church, was it you?" I questioned calmly as I prepared myself within.

I'd never been in a fight before as I had never been in a situation where it was needed, seeing as though I never had any friends or went to school or anything. I'd been swatted and smacked around by my grandmother when she had a little more steam in her, but I'd never had to hit anyone before.

"That freak, the freak with the metal leg?" he questioned as his friends laughed.

I don't know what happened for the next few minutes after that but everything went black. When I came to, Nicky and his two friends were huddled over on their hands and knees in what sounded like pain and agony, grunting and groaning.

I walked over to the dog and slowly petted it as I untied the rope from around its neck. It was cowering with its head hanging low and shivering quite bad. I took my shirt off and wrapped it around the dogs' body. It was a pretty shaggy looking dog, not more than a few years old and medium sized. As I picked it up to carry it, it whimpered just once then didn't make another sound.

"I better not hear of you hurtin' nobody no more...not even no poor dog," I stated quite confidently, even though I was still unsure of what happened.

The boys were just getting to their feet as I walked by them with the dog cuddled up against my bare belly, straddling my arms; they didn't say anything nor did I mutter another word.

I headed home.

Walking home, gripping on to the young pup cradled in my arms as I leaned back to keep my balance, it didn't do much more than let out a deep breath every few minutes as its head hung over my arms, watching the passing ground below.

When I got back to the house Hope was outside swinging from the tire that Mr. Charlie had tied to the tree, next to the garden, for me years ago. She had her legs strung through the tire as she sat comfortably on the plank that Mr. Charlie had constructed; she appeared to be in better spirits.

"Who you got there?" she asked curiously as she smiled.

"This my new friend," I answered, smiling back as I walked toward her.

"He got a name?" she asked playfully.

"Not yet, don't even know if he a boy," I said as I slowly dropped to my knees to put the puppy on the ground.

"Awe, he cute, can we name him?" she questioned as she wiggled out of the tire swing and came to sit next to the puppy and me.

I peeled my shirt from underneath its belly as it laid shivering on the grass while Hope began to pet it from one end to the other; it closed its eyes in what appeared to be complete relaxation.

"See, he is a boy...let's name 'im," she said quickly, smiling with excitement.

"Go on then, you name him," I answered happily.

"For real? I ain't never gave nothin' no name before," she stated shyly.

Hope stared at the puppy as she continued to pet it while I could see her mind wandering off in search of the perfect name.

"Where'd you find him?" she asked curiously.

"Down by the church," I answered without hesitation.

"Hmmm...." she started. "How 'bout, Lucky?" she asked, smiling from ear to ear.

I couldn't have picked a more appropriate name for him, under the circumstances of how he had found his way into our company.

"I like that," I said, giggling, as I petted our new friend.

"Wait here," she said as she slowly made her way to her feet before going toward the house.

I laid on the grass under the tree next to Lucky, enjoying the shade while we waited for Hope. He was still shivering and his breathing had a seemingly nervous rhythm to it. Every few minutes he would open his eye and roll it around until he found his focus on me, and then he'd close it again slowly.

Hope came outside along with Ms. Violet, each carrying a bowl.

"Oh, well isn't he jus a sweetheart," Ms. Violet chirped with joy as she set the bowl of water down in front of Lucky.

Hope set down her bowl filled with chicken guts, which Ms. Violet kindly warmed quickly over the stove, that would've normally found its way tossed out back at the edge of the bush, but would now become Lucky's first meal with us. Her and Ms. Violet made their way down to the grass alongside Lucky and me and began to pet him as they tried to entice him into some food or drink. He didn't budge, although he did appear to be somewhat enjoying the attention through the gentle petting which he was receiving. His eye, as he laid on one side, was spending more time open than it had been just a few minutes before.

"Where he gonna sleep at?" Hope asked me as she leaned on one hand, continuing to pet Lucky with the other.

"This your pup now?" Ms. Violet asked me.

"Yeah, think so, he's mine, but mostly he gonna be mine and Hopes' pup from now on. Don't know where he gonna sleep though, might have to sneak him past grandma after she in bed," I answered, snickering at the very thought of doing so.

"Now don't you go doin' nothin' that be sure to catch you a whoopin'," Ms. Violet insisted as she smiled, knowing how my grandmother would most certainly react to finding a dog in her house.

"I ain't, I'm jus foolin; I'll find him a place to sleep, he be fine," I said in return.

"He'll be fine," Ms. Violet stated, accentuating her words.

"Yes ma'am...*he'll*," I returned, correcting myself.

The three of us sat petting Lucky while we laughed and played with each other. Every so often Hope would show a slight discomfort and slowly shift her body to accommodate her leg as Ms. Violet would attempt to help. Hope clearly didn't like any attention being brought to her leg so every time Ms. Violet would reach to help, Hope would just give her a look and Ms. Violet would retract her gesture. I could see that it hurt Ms. Violet to watch Hope in pain, as well as not be able to do anything to help her. She was a strong woman and rarely showed any emotion outside of love, but this, I could see bothered her as her mood became visibly dampened and she soon stood to her feet.

"How's about some lemonade?" Ms. Violet asked as she whipped the towel she had draped over her shoulder against her dress to rid it of any grass that had clung to it.

"Yes please, ma'am," I answered.

"Sugar?" Ms. Violet asked of Hope.

"Please," Hope replied in short.

Ms. Violet was quickly back in our company, under the shade of the tree, with three tall glasses of freshly made lemonade, along with a cookie for each of us. We took a break from smothering Lucky with our heavy-handed petting to relax and sip on our cool beverage, while enjoying some of Ms. Violet's fine baking.

"So jus where'd you find this poor young thing anyway?" Ms. Violet asked of me.

"Down by the church," I answered quickly.

"The church?" she asked.

"Yes ma'am, the church," I replied as I took a bite of my cookie.

"Well ain't that sumthin' else," she said in wonder.

"What is, ma'am?" I questioned, curiously.

"Even a puppy, small and pain stricken as this, can be found for savin' right in Gods' own backyard; the very same place people been meetin' for years to find a savin' for they 'selves," she said as she looked to the sky, smiling.

Lucky appeared to be drifting off into sleep as Hope had begun lovingly petting his fragile young, four-legged frame, while Ms. Violet spoke of *'the glory of God'*. She never forced any interaction or even her own beliefs when she spoke of God, she just had a place in her heart that was filled with a love, surely out of this world, for the God in whom she often spoke of. I never made an effort to clear any space in my young heart for any firm belief or even disbelief in God, but I was always in awe of the love that Ms. Violet carried around in her voice when she would go on speaking of **him**. Hope, however, didn't seem too keen on listening to much of it as she had her attention buried in her new found affection for Lucky.

The three of us sat together for a while longer, until Ms. Violet went to fix supper, just as my grandmother stuck her head out the back window of the house, calling me to come and eat.

"Guess I gotta go...can you watch him 'till I'm done?" I asked of Hope as I stood to my feet.

"Yeah, 'course I can," she said, smiling as she slid down on her side next to Lucky, resting her head on one arm.

I watched Hope lay with him on the grass as I washed my hands in the rain barrel out back before heading into the house. I smiled to myself as I was happy to have found two new friends, both of whom were within a spitting distance from where I slept. Life, surprisingly by the day, was increasingly getting better.

"What'd you do to your shirt?" my grandmother grumbled as I sat down at the supper table.

Looking down, I tugged at the front of my shirt and I could see it was torn and covered in streaks of dirt from having Lucky wrapped in it on the walk back from the church.

"Umm...I 'uh, I dunno, ma'am, looks like it tore," I replied hesitantly.

"Well I can see that," she snarled. "You gone thick or sumthin'?" she went on, glaring at me.

My grandmother would often refer to people who she felt had no sense as being *thick*. It was her way of calling someone dumb without having to say it.

"No ma'am," I replied softly.

I didn't want to tell her about Lucky just yet as I could see she was already in a bad mood and I didn't want to make it any worse.

"You got a stash 'uh clothes somewhere I don't know about that gives you the freedom to ruin what 'chu got...what I already done given you?" she prodded, annoyed.

"No ma'am, jus got this one and the one more," I answered, looking down at my shirt as I tugged at it.

"How you suppose you gonna patch that...fix that up?" she asked, squinting, as she put her cigarette down to take a bite of food.

"I dunno, ma'am, could ask Ms. Violet I guess," I suggested, positive that I had just solved the problem.

"Nah, you ain't doin' that...you gonna go and you gonna fix that on your own; you ain't runnin' around askin' people to fix somethin' for you, somethin' that you went and ruined yourself," she stated calmly, reaching for her cigarette.

"Yes ma'am," I answered softly.

We sat quietly beside each other as my grandmother continued to inhale long drags of her cigarette in between bites of her meal. I often had to cough from the lingering smoke but tried to do so under my breath, otherwise she would send me outside to eat on the back steps, making it quite clear just whose home I was in. Most often it would depend on the weather outside on just how loud my coughing would get; I would tend to exaggerate my cough during the summer as it was always a pleasant break to eat alone, even if it was outside on the steps.

"Where you think you off to?" my grandmother asked as I stood up from the table once I finished eating.

"Was thinkin' jus next door, ma'am, to visit," I replied without question.

"Not like that you ain't, you best get to fixin' that damn shirt you wearin'," she demanded, waving her burning cigarette around.

My grandmother got up from the table and went into her bedroom; she came back out with a needle, some thread, a pair of scissors, and what looked like an old torn up towel.

"There yah go...get to it," she said as she set it all down on the kitchen table.

I didn't know the first thing about sewing and I had a mind full of other things I'd rather be doing with my evening, but it was clear that I wasn't going to so much as step outside until I fixed my shirt.

My grandmother sat back down at the table as I peeled my shirt up and over my head, removing it from my body. She continued to eat, slowly, between long drags from her cigarette as she verbally walked me through each step, beginning with threading the tiny eye of the needle with what seemed to be some very oversized thread which she had given to me.

"Wet it...jus get it in between your lips and wet the thread so the end sticks...you'll see," she explained, pointing, with one eye closed.

I did as she said and it worked.

"See, what I say?" she barked.

"Yes ma'am, you said it and, and you was right," I answered quietly.

By the time I was finished patching my shirt half the evening had passed by. I was eager to get outside and see how Lucky was doing as well as visit with Hope before it was time for bed.

Hope and Mr. Charlie were out back setting down some fresh water and scraps from supper for Lucky just as I came outside. Ms. Violet was right behind them with an old, ragged blanket in her hands from inside the house; she was smiling from ear to ear as she approached the young pup.

"Evening, my young brother, I see you brought us a new friend," Mr. Charlie spoke out as I anxiously approached them.

"Yes sir, he was hurtin' pretty bad when I found him. He lookin' any better?" I replied curiously.

"Ah, he'll be fine, I'm sure of it, he got that look in his eyes," he said, smiling proudly as he looked down at Lucky.

"Sweetheart, what happened to 'ur poor little fingers?" Ms. Violet asked of me.

"I torn my shirt, ma'am...then grandma had me patch it," I said as I tugged on my shirt to show her my sewing job.

Each fingertip on my left hand was bandaged up, quite poorly, as I did it myself, from the repeated pricking of the needle as I did my best to sew a piece of an old dish towel over the tear on my shirt.

The appearance of my bandage job was far worse than what was underneath but it was all I could do on my own, with my opposite hand, while my grandmother watched me use small pieces of the leftover towel to stop the bleeding.

"Hey, Hope," I said, smiling at her as I waved my bandaged hand.

"Hi," she replied softly, as she smiled while she petted Lucky.

I crouched down next to Hope and extended my hand to gently pet our new friend while Ms. Violet and Mr. Charlie stood nearby, both with smiles stretched across their faces, as he wrapped his arm around her.

Lucky was snuggled up under the large tree in the blanket that Ms. Violet had given him, while his food and water bowls were both within reach of his hopeful snout. He looked to be in better spirits as the four of us said goodnight to each other and went off to our homes.

Chapter 5

When I got in, my grandmother was already in bed so I went in to check on her and say goodnight like I often did. She was sound asleep on top of her blankets with a cigarette still burning in the ashtray beside her bed, and her bible folded open across her chest. I butted out the cigarette, as I'd done many times before, then I pulled the blanket up from her feet and over her sleeping body. I said a short prayer in thanks, kissed her on her cheek, and went out into the kitchen.

After putting a pot of water on the stove to boil, so I could soak my clothes overnight, I sat down at the kitchen table to wait. I had just bit into an apple when I heard a yelping coming from outside. I slid a chair across the kitchen floor and stood on it to get a better look out the back window but it was too dark, I couldn't see anything. As the noise got louder and more concerning, I slid my grandmothers' slippers on at the back door and cautiously made my way outside toward the noise. As I neared the sound it became clear that it was Lucky. He was wrapped up in his old blanket and couldn't find his way out. Panicking under the light of the full moon, he was tossing and turning as he continued to cry out, in search of an exit. I stood over him laughing for a few moments before I relieved him of his anguish. Standing under the canopy of the large tree in nothing but my grandmothers' slippers and my underwear, Lucky and I shared a few minutes of calming relief before I made my way back into the house.

While I walked away Lucky was whimpering softly and just as I neared the house I could see that the kitchen window was steamed up. Suddenly remembering that I had left the pot of water on the stove to boil I began to run the last few steps into the house. When I got to the stove the pot was bone dry, all of the water had disappeared. I shut the stove off with a sigh of relief and I went to bed.

I woke up the next morning to the sound of a wooden spoon clanging and banging against the inside of a pot, right next to my head. Opening my eyes in a sense of panicked daze, my grandmother began to shout at me.

"What 'chu done to my pot, Poor Boy...and don't 'chu go on explainin' like you ain't done nothin', I know you done burnt the damn bottom out of it!" she spoke loudly, quite angry.

"Yes, ma'am, I, I did that, I burnt that pot," I answered softly as I cringed, expecting to receive a swat from the wooden spoon she was gripping.

"What was you thinkin'...you think we got so much that it ain't no big deal if you jus run around burnin' things up and tearin' up jus about the only clothes you got?" she demanded.

"No ma'am, I wasn't...I wasn't thinkin' like that...I jus..." I stammered.

"You jus what, Poor-Boy...dammit, you jus what?" she raised her voice.

"I was jus tryin' to wash my clothes is all, and then I heard a noise outside so I went to see what it was...when I got back all the water was gone from the pot, it jus disappeared...*I swear on it!*" I explained with sincerity as I raised my hands.

"It jus disappeared?! You one lucky little...what if you woulda gone and burnt the whole damn house down, huh, where you gonna go then, 'cause I know for certain you outta people who want you...'specially if you burnin' down kitchens," she shouted.

"I'm sorry, ma'am, I really am, I wasn't thinkin' like that," I said as I propped myself up, still under my blanket.

"Now I know you wasn't thinkin', child, that's the whole problem with you, you **never** thinkin'," she belted as she turned and walked into the kitchen, slamming the pot on the counter.

I slowly got off the couch and folded up my blanket, leaving it and my pillow on the floor. I got dressed; putting on the same clothes I wore the day before, and went to wash up.

When I walked into the kitchen my grandmother was still scowling at me so I just kept on walking, right out the back door. I knew that look and it meant *'get outta my sight',* so I did just that.

"Mornin", Poor Boy!" Mr. Charlie belted out across the yard with a bucket hanging from his large hand.

As he reached Lucky he dumped the bucket filled with fresh water into the freshly excitable young dogs' bowl. Lucky was dancing around, appearing to be chasing his own behind, as Mr. Charlie spoke to him.

I walked over to see them.

"Morning, sir, everything alright?" I asked, smiling, as I squinted against the rising sun.

"Everything jus fine, son, everything jus fiiiine," he replied, smiling, with a slow and cheerful tone.

"And a good mornin' to you my friend," I chirped as I bent over and cupped Lucky's face in my hands.

"Girls' in the house, they jus fixin' some breakfast, if you hungry," Mr. Charlie explained.

"Good mornin', sweetheart, you come on in and sit down, Sugar jus settin' a place for you now…she spotted you from the window," Ms. Violet shouted from the back steps.

"Yes ma'am, be right there," I answered back as I waved.

"Those girls' is sure fond 'uh you, we all are, you know that…and you need to keep that close in 'ur heart, right there," Mr. Charlie said, kindly, as he poked me in the chest.

"Yes sir, thank you, sir," I said shyly.

"Ain't no thanks about it, son, no thanks needed…you a fine young man, one that *any* father be proud to claim, no doubt," he stated, smiling, as he nodded at me.

I stood still for a minute; I wasn't sure what to say. A tear began to run down my cheek just as Lucky jumped up at me, playfully wanting my attention.

"Hey, boy…I see you, I ain't forget you was here," I said, snapping out of my daze as I wiped my cheek clean of tears.

"You'll be fine, son, you gonna be alright, I can see it in your eyes…always have, since you was jus a baby…you got that look, same as this here pup got in him," Mr. Charlie insisted as he gripped onto my shoulder.

"I best go on and get in the house now, sir, thank you for…." I started.

"You go on…go eat 'n enjoy your day," he said, smiling.

"Have a good day, Mr. Charlie," I said as I turned and walked toward the house.

I looked back and he appeared to be saying his goodbyes to Lucky for the day as he was energetically petting him while he spoke to him. Mr. Charlie looked over at me, smiled and waved, then stood up straight, grabbed his lunch pail and walked off. Lucky was whimpering as he watched Mr. Charlie leave his line of sight. He didn't change his focus on Mr. Charlie for as long as I stood there to watch, before I went into the house.

"Sit child, sit, your food's gettin' a chill," Ms. Violet said with a soft, loving tone.

Hope was already seated at the table, slowly picking away at her breakfast. She smiled at me and I smiled back as I pulled out my chair to sit next to her where she had set my plate.

The three of us enjoyed our breakfast together as we sat visiting, sharing stories and laughing at how noisy Lucky was the night before. They were surprised to know that it was me who had went outside to calm him. I sat, smiling shyly with pride as they were both speaking so kindly of me.

After being woken up so abruptly and scolded by my grandmother, the morning had certainly turned around.

When I was all finished eating and Ms. Violet began to clean up, I requested her help in removing the pieces of cloth I still had tied around my fingertips. She continued to clean up after us and handed Hope a pair of scissors to assist me.

Nervously, I sat with my hand hanging over the edge of the kitchen table as Hope began to gently cut the small pieces of string off each of my fingertips, allowing the cloth to fall freely onto the floor below.

Ms. Violet handed Hope a bowl and told her to grab the jar of honey from the pantry while she put some water on to boil as I cleaned up the bits of cloth off the table and floor.

When the water came to a boil Ms. Violet scooped a large glob of honey out of the jar and slapped it into the bowl, followed by the hot water; to speed up the dissolving of the honey she had Hope stir it around the bowl. After a few minutes, the honey was completely dissolved and the water had cooled just slightly, Ms. Violet then firmly grabbed my hand and gently eased it into the bowl.

"There, you keep that soak until I say so," she commanded, before going back to the countertop where she was mixing her ingredients to make bread.

"Why you soakin' his hand in honey water?" Hope asked of Ms. Violet, seemingly confused.

"We jus gonna sweeten him up...*jus a little,*" she replied, smiling, not missing a beat.

"For real?" Hope returned, innocently.

"Yes, for real," Ms. Violet said quickly. "Don't you think he could use a little mo' sweetness?" she questioned Hope as she winked at me.

I smiled back at Ms. Violet then chuckled lightly as I looked over at Hope, shrugging my shoulders, while my hand was still dunked into the steaming bowl of honey water.

Hope looked at Ms. Violet and then back at me, unsure of how to respond.

"You jus foolin' me, he ain't gonna get no sweeter jus by stickin' his hand in no bowl," Hope spoke with a matter of fact tone as she waved her hand to dismiss Ms. Violet's remark.

"It's jus to take care of any infections or anything that might try 'n set in on him. Jus a good cleanin' is all, he already jus about as sweet as any young boy can get...ain't he?" Ms. Violet explained as she smiled back at me from the sink just a few feet away.

After about ten minutes of my hand soaking and the playful banter back and forth between the three of us, Ms. Violet pulled my hand out and dried it off with the towel that she had draped over her shoulder. Hope was standing, leaning against the back of a chair at the kitchen table while Ms. Violet handed her the bowl to dump into the sink.

"Thank you, ma'am," I said to Ms. Violet as she suffocated my hand in the towel, playfully taking her time.

"You're welcome, my love," she replied softly, releasing my hand from her grip.

"Wanna go outside?" I asked of Hope.

"Sure...that okay?" Hope replied as she looked to Ms. Violet.

"Of course, Sugar, you go on, you two go out 'n enjoy the sun," she answered Hope with a chirp in her voice, smiling.

I quickly stood up, tucked my chair in and set out the back door behind Hope.

Walking outside, as soon as we were in sight of Lucky he began to whimper. Hope picked up her pace and set off toward him, talking to him along the way. He was tied loosely to the tree with an old shredded rope that surely wouldn't take him too long to gnaw his way through, if he set his mind to it. Instead, he insisted on running out the slack and jumping into the air, forcing himself to be pulled backward once the slack tightened. It was funny to watch and even more so because it was so nice to see him find his energy and happiness after how he had originally been when I first found him. Ms. Violet was against having him tied up but Mr. Charlie said it would be best just until he was used to this being his home, and then he wouldn't need it.

Hope was quick to grab on to him and do her best to calm his increasingly wild energy.

He was acting like this young boy, one in particular, quite smaller than me, from church, who always seemed to have more energy than he knew what to do with. *"He need to be dropped off in the middle 'uh the lake and left to swim until he tires' out or sinks"*, is how my grandmother put it when the child wouldn't settle down for an entire service. Lucky's sudden energy was much the same.

"Should we take him for a walk?" I asked Hope as she was trying to tame him.

"Okay," she replied, shrugging her shoulders, not taking her eyes off of him.

I patted Lucky on the head then walked over to the tree and untied the rope. As I wrapped the rope around my waist and tied it, Hope continued to pet and talk to him. She was very kind and patient with her words and her touch. For as hyper as he was my ability to brush it off wasn't anything like her effort in making him feel at ease. Lucky was tugging on the rope, which in turn was yanking on my waist and all I could do was laugh as I watched Hope stay determined in helping him pay attention to her instructions before she would allow us to go.

"Quit laughing, you jus makin' it worse, he jus doin' it now to make you laugh," she lectured me.

"Okay, Lucky, cut it out, we wanna go," I said in favor of Hope's demand.

Lucky planted his behind in the dirt and sat still; Hope looked at me and rolled her eyes, shaking her head.

"He was listenin' to you," I suggested as I pointed at Lucky, raising my eyebrows in an effort to sell it with surprise.

"He wasn't payin' no mind to nobody, he jus tired his self out is all," she said, annoyed with the situation.

"Nah, he ain't tired, he ain't never gonna tire...he jus wanna go," I replied playfully.

The three of us set out on our way. Hope continued her light banter with Lucky, talking softly to him about our surroundings, helping to familiarize him with his new environment. He appeared to be listening as he keenly looked around while she spoke to him. I didn't say too much because every time I opened my mouth Hope scowled at me, much like my grandmother would, as though I was interrupting her teachings only meant for Lucky; she was funny. I would just smile to myself in pleasure of being able to be in her company, as she would talk to Lucky and he would tug on my waist, then she would roll her eyes at me for anything outside of me walking at her desired pace.

As we entered the edge of the forest, Hope suggested that we untie Lucky and let him run freely; so I did. Without a second to blink Lucky took off running; he was ducking and dodging, over and under, smiling from ear to ear as he whipped around the trees. Hope and I both broke out laughing as we watched him with his tongue hanging out while his fur flapped up and down against his young frame with each stride that he took.

"He runnin' like he ain't never been free," I said as I smiled with delight in watching him.

"Yeah, he sure a new dog from jus a day ago…he look like he found his'self," Hope added.

Hope and I continued walking deeper into the forest as Lucky kept up with us, then he'd run ahead, circle around, and come up from behind; he seemed to have a never ending source of energy within his little body.

The sound of birds singing back and forth to each other throughout the trees above was a quick reminder of the peace I used to seek on my own not so long ago. With every step we took among the beauty that surrounded us, the squeaking of the hinges on Hopes' leg brace seemed to stand out more and more.

"What's the matter?" I asked as she stopped walking.

"You hear that?" she asked, looking up at the sky.

"Hear what?" I replied, as I did the same.

"There a creek nearby?" she asked softly.

"Jus over that way," I said, pointing.

She began walking in the direction to which I pointed. I stood still for a few minutes watching her as Lucky followed her lead with all of his trust, at her side. Running to catch up to her I tripped over a branch. Hope looked back just as I stood to my feet, as quickly as I could.

"You gonna get it now I bet," Hope said giggling as she pointed to my shirt.

"Awe jus great," I exclaimed as I looked down to see that the patch fell off and the front of my shirt was torn again.

"You ain't gonna fix that one, Poor Boy, you may as well jus leave that rag where she ain't never gonna find it," Hope suggested, quite amused.

"You about right, but I bet she gonna gimme a whoopin' for it this time," I said as I peeled the shirt off my sweaty body.

"She whoop you?" Hope asked gently.

"If she need to," I answered simply.

"It don't bother you none?" she asked, looking at me, seeming confused.

"I don't care for it much but it's how she say it gotta be from time to time," I explained with ease.

"You jus take it?" she questioned.

"She done her best with somethin' she ain't never wanted to begin with, so if she gotta whoop me every now 'n again...ain't no point in me fussin'," I said as I tucked my shirt under a pile of leaves next to a fallen tree.

"You sumthin' else..." Hope said as she smiled and shook her head.

"What 'chu mean by that?" I asked curiously as I stood to my feet.

"You jus are is all...I ain't never met nobody like you before," she replied, smiling.

"Yeah, well, there ain't but one of each of us, so I guess it jus meant to be that we neighbors now," I said as I picked up a stick and batted it against the tree.

"What 'chu doin' now?" she questioned curiously.

"Jus tryin' to remember what tree I'm leavin' my shirt by," I answered as I continued to smack the tree.

"How you gonna do that?" she asked as she scrunched her face in disbelief.

"By the echo it leaves in the forest. The weather 'n all gotta be near the same but I'll find it, no doubt...if I need to," I said, scratching my bare belly after I gave the tree one last whack.

"You full of it," she belted, mocking me.

"You watch, we can come back another way, or tomorrow or the next day, and I'll find it, jus like that," I explained with confidence.

"Yeah...we'll see," she stated simply.

We continued on, as I took the lead, in the direction of the creek. We shared moments without talking but were never short of things to say. I would whistle and she would try to join in harmony but instead would blow mostly tuneless air. I didn't so much as crack a smile at her for not being able to whistle; in fact, for me it made more sense that she couldn't. She was so pretty and seemed perfect in so many other ways that not being able to whistle was the one thing that kept her human in my eyes.

Just as we came to a break in the trees that opened to the creek, the sun beat down on us with all of its might. I didn't hesitate; I ran in knee deep and began to splash my bare belly and face. Hope slipped off her shoes and slowly walked in just past her ankles while she held her dress up above her knees.

"Where'd Lucky go?" Hope asked, slightly concerned.

"Lucky!" I shouted.

We went back and forth taking turns yelling his name.

"I wonder where he took off to?" Hope asked, looking around.

"He jus up to no good somewhere...watch, he gonna come out runnin' in no time," I said with certainty.

Sure enough, before he poked his oversized head out under the sun, we could begin to hear the slapping and snapping of branches as he was surely in full stride heading toward our voices.

"Heeey boy, there you are! Where was you hiding at?" Hope welcomed him as she threw her hands up in the air, leaving the bottom of her dress free to surf in the slow moving water below.

"What's he got in his mouth?" I asked as he got closer.

Hope burst out laughing.

"Looks like you ain't the only one in tune with the *echoes of the forest*, Poor Boy," she teased, continuing to laugh.

"Awe nooo, Lucky, that wasn't supposed to be found by you, boy, I was stashin' that from grandma," I said, joining in Hope's laughter.

"Well at least we know he got a good nose on 'em," Hope chirped, still laughing.

We continued to laugh as I praised Lucky for bringing me my shirt, then I took it from him and buried it in the bank along the water. Lucky and I splashed around for a little while longer as Hope stayed at ankle depth, kicking water at us. The three of us were becoming great friends.

My stomach began to call to me and Hope was complaining of thirst, so we made our way back through the forest toward home.

Hope was trying to teach Lucky how to play fetch while we walked, so any urgency we once had to get home to quench our hunger and thirst quickly went out the window in exchange for her effort to have him retrieve a stick. It was quite amusing to watch her give him directions because he clearly enjoyed causing her grief and she was very adamant about not stopping until he "got it". I did my best not to bud in and show her up because he and I seemed to have an understanding with each other, where he would simply do as I asked, and it bothered Hope to witness. She'd look over at me every few minutes while she waited for Lucky to find it in his little heart to return the stick, then she'd give me this look, and I knew exactly what it meant so I'd just throw my hands up in the air in a playful surrender. Meanwhile, Lucky would run up to her as if he was coming to obey her teeth gritting request, then shoot off in a circle around her and off again into the distance. As bad as I wanted to feed my growling stomach, I was more than happy with watching Lucky have his way with the already short and now lit fuse of Hope's temper.

I sat down with my back against a tree and smiled to myself as I was so happy to have my new, and first ever, friends.

Hope began to walk and I soon got up to follow her lead home. Her and Lucky continued their back and forth for the remainder of our travels toward the house. As soon as she acted as though she didn't care, Lucky would surrender the stick. She soon caught on to his little game then she just ended up holding onto the stick and not giving in to him.

"You got yourself a reason for losin' your shirt?" Hope asked as we were getting ready to part ways.

"It ain't gonna make much difference," I answered simply.

"See you after dinner?" she asked.

"See you after dinner," I replied.

Later that evening, after catching a good whooping from my grandmother and eating my dinner on the back step, I cleaned up and went outside to see Lucky.

I left some meat on the bone from my dinner and tucked it beside the steps until I was able to get it to him. He was more than happy just to be noticed, but he was sure in love with that bone. He licked my face from chin to hair line and then didn't pay another moments' notice to me. I watched him for a little while until Mr. Charlie came outside.

"Evenin' son," he said as he approached, taking a long drag on his pipe.

"Good evenin', Mr. Charlie, how's things?" I welcomed him.

"Everything is alright, everything…everythin' is real good," he replied with a smile and a wink. "You gonna catch a chill," he suggested as he pointed to my bare upper body.

"No, sir, I'll be fine…thank you," I answered looking up at him as Lucky was still gnawing at his bone next to me.

"You know, she do love you, son, don't you ever think she don't…she jus too worn out to show you proper is all," he said, pointing in the direction of my grandmothers' house with his still smoking pipe.

"Yes sir…in another time maybe," I suggested as it became apparent that he'd overheard my grandmother giving me a thrashing.

"Loneliness'll do curious things to a persons' mind…real curious things…but then, so will love; she jus lost her balance is all," he stated with compassion.

"Yes sir," I replied.

"Now when you come to find a good woman, who got a good soul, a good heart…one who keep you on your toes…you jus hold on like you ain't got no choice, like your every breath depend on it. And hey, you gotta let'er be, you gotta let'er be herself, and jus accept her craziness…'cause they all *jus a bit crazy*…but 'chu need that, it keeps the fire burnin'. *And you gotta love that woman hard*, with all your heart, everything you got, each and every day you get to have her; you make it so that even *death itself* ain't got no say," he explained with passion as he poked my bare chest with his index finger while he clenched his hand around his pipe.

"Yes sir," I said simply.

"Can you promise me that, son?" he asked proudly.

"Yes sir, I can promise," I answered softly.

"Well, lemme hear it then," he said with enthusiasm as he shuffled his feet in a little dance.

"I promise, sir...I promise I'm gonna love my woman so strong that even death will want some," I stumbled.

"Ha ha ha you alright, Poor Boy, you young yet, you young, but 'chu gonna get it. You keep those words I jus give to you and you remember 'em, remember 'em, and you gonna be jus fine in love one day," he insisted, chuckling, as he relit his pipe.

The two of us sat outside visiting next to Lucky while Mr. Charlie continued to smoke and then repack his pipe with his thumb. I loved the smell of burning tobacco and I would often stretch my neck just to reach his blowing smoke.

I didn't see Hope that evening; Ms. Violet said that she had fallen asleep right after dinner, after spending most of her time at the table talking about what a fun day she had. I smiled as I thought of Hope, and her stubborn little heart, sharing in the joy of her day.

Chapter 6

I woke up the next morning to the sound of my grandmother singing in the kitchen. I was stunned for a few minutes as I tried to get my wits about me, but I instead chose to surrender to the sweet sounds of her voice, so I closed my eyes and laid still. She was cooking breakfast as she sang, skipping through different hymns that were often saved, exclusively, for church.

Beyond the moment, I couldn't think of a single time that I'd heard my grandmother singing in the house; it just wasn't something that she did, at least not when I was around.

I opened my eyes just enough to see her through my eyelashes. Her back was to me, she was wearing one of her nicer dresses and she had an apron tied around her waist. As she continued to sing she was moving her head in rhythm along with her hips and shuffling feet. I pulled my blanket up to my nose so I could keep a better eye on her without being detected. As I filled my blanket with the warm air from my breath, I continued to watch and listen to her. I was smiling, knowing that no matter how hard she would ever whoop me again I could take it, because she really was the presence of love, and there was no disputing that when I heard her sing.

"You up?" my grandmother belted.

"Yes ma'am," I answered as I sat up.

"Well, c'mon then, before it cools," she said as she looked at me while she set the table in the next room.

"Comin' ma'am, jus gonna put my bedding away," I replied as I scurried around the couch.

"You jus leave all that for now, come 'n sit," she insisted with a light tone.

"Yes ma'am," I said as I made my way into the kitchen.

"Sit, sit," she said softly, pointing to my plate.

I sat down then she sat beside me just a few moments later. I caught the scent of her perfume as she put her hand over mine and slowly nodded at me in a gesture of grace.

"Heavenly Father, thank you for the food we 'bout to receive, and thank you Father for my grandson, he always mean well and he been a real blessing to this small and humble home, which you done given to us...amen," she ran over the words as if they were no stranger to her tongue.

As she spoke I could feel her intention while she slowly gripped my hand.

"Amen," I said in short, smiling at her.

The two of us sat beside each other eating slowly, sharing very few words. After she said grace there wasn't much left to say. I was thankful for her surrender in words and I didn't feel like the moment needed any prodding so I was more than happy just to enjoy her pancakes and quiet, but pleasant, company.

After breakfast, my grandmother and I washed and dried dishes together. She insisted on doing them herself but since it was the first time I had the chance to do them next to her, ever since I was big enough to stand on a chair and do them myself, I sloughed it off and helped. Our banter was light as we giggled while the morning sun shined through the kitchen window.

Once we were done I went outside to see Lucky.

I could hear the deep rumble of Mr. Charlie's voice as I walked out the back door; he was outside feeding Lucky as he spoke to him. I didn't pay any attention to what he was saying I was just happy to see the two of them.

"Mornin' Mr. Charlie," I yelped as I approached him kneeling over Lucky.

"Ha ha good mornin' my young friend," he said in return with a joyful tone.

"Mornin' boy, I see you...you musta' slept all night, boy, I didn't hear a peep...not nothin' outta you," I said cheerfully as Lucky left his breakfast to welcome me with kisses.

"I think our new friend is findin' his'self a welcome home, and he startin' to get good 'n comfortable," Mr. Charlie spoke out as he watched over Lucky and I greet each other.

"Sure do look that way, don't it?" I replied, smiling with great joy.

Mr. Charlie and I played around with Lucky as we visited with each other for a short while longer, until Hope made her way outside to say hello.

"Even the sun itself couldn't help but come out from behind the clouds to see what all the fuss about," Mr. Charlie said proudly as Hope came outside.

"Good mornin', Hope," I said as I stood, topless, in bare feet next to Mr. Charlie.

"Mornin', Poor Boy," she replied as she squinted against the sun.

Mr. Charlie walked toward her and gave her a kiss on the forehead as he went to give Ms. Violet a hand with the laundry baskets that she was carrying outside to hang on the line.

Hope came over and said a very gentle and quiet "good morning" to Lucky as she appeared to be in a very timid mood.

The day passed with a very similar energy to that of Hope's mood.

My grandmother was back and forth between the garden and the house for most of the day. I helped her do some light weeding in the garden as Hope sat off to the side with Lucky and watched. My grandmother was making an effort in small talk with Hope as she was bent over pulling weeds, before tossing them in between the rows for me to pick up.

That evening, when I was done visiting next door and finished up with supper I went home. When I walked in the house it was filled with the smell of fresh baking, and on the kitchen table was a big, round, fluffy, chocolate covered cake. In front of it was a piece of paper with writing on it; it read "Happy Birthday, Enjoy. Love Grandma".

I was so excited I didn't know what to do with myself. I had never tasted a chocolate cake before, but I did see one after church once at my grandmothers' friends' house; they were all sharing it amongst themselves while they played cards, although I wasn't allowed to have any, and now here I was with a whole cake in front of me along with a note telling me that it was my birthday. And a great thanks to Ms. Violet's persistent teachings, I was able to sound it out and read the note all on my own.

I poked my head around the corner into my grandmothers' room to check on her but she was already sound asleep. I walked to her bedside, pulled up her blanket and set her bible on her nightstand next to her ashtray, then I kissed her on the cheek, said a short prayer in thanks and left her room.

I went back into the kitchen and sat at the table, staring at the cake. I knew what needed to be done; I picked up the dish with the cake set on top and I quietly made my way outside.

Lucky was whimpering for my attention as I passed him; I said hello but didn't stop.

With the cake leaning against my chest I knocked on the back door of my neighbors' home.

"Thought you was done for the night, gone home to bed?" Ms. Violet enquired as she opened the door.

"I was, ma'am, but then I got in and this was waitin' for me, so I thought I'd come share it with ya'll since grandma, well, she already sound asleep," I explained, smiling from ear to ear.

"Well where'd you come across such a thing?" she asked cheerfully.

"Grandma made it for me...she even left a note sayin' that it's my *birthday,*" I returned with pride and joy.

"Your birthday? Well I'll be...you best get in here then!" she yelped as she pried open the back door.

"Thank you, ma'am," I said as I ducked under her arm to walk in.

"C'mon ya'll, we got a guest...and it turns out, it's the young mans' birthday!" Ms. Violet shouted into the house as she closed the door behind her.

Mr. Charlie and Hope came out into the kitchen, both with curious smiles.

"Now jus what 'chu got there, Poor Boy?" Mr. Charlie asked, smiling.

"A chocolate cake, sir, I come to share it...if you be so kind to have some with me?" I replied joyfully.

"If I be so kind?" he asked, laughing. "Son, you welcome to show up at any hour if you bringin' big 'ol cakes with you...what's that, chocolate?" he rambled, playfully.

"Yes, sir, chocolate...it'll be my first taste," I replied, smiling, as I held on to the cake.

"First taste?" he asked.

"And, Hope, since I know we the same, with no real birthday to be had...I figured we could jus share it, you know...have it be both our birthdays," I stumbled through my offering.

"Now ain't that somethin'," Mr. Charlie said as he smiled, resting his hand on the shoulder of Hope.

"I couldn't think 'uh nothin' better," Ms. Violet chirped with joy as she clapped her hands together just once.

Hope just stood still, smiling shyly.

The four of us sat down and enjoyed ourselves; it was the best thing I'd ever tasted. I ate two pieces and the second was even better than the first. Hope quietly ate just one piece, but did so with a smile throughout each tiny bite.

We laughed a lot, visiting, and listening to Mr. Charlie's stories until late into the night as we ate birthday cake in celebration of mine and Hope's first official birthday.

I saved the last piece on the plate for my grandmother, which everyone at the table had insisted the same.

After we finished cleaning up and saying goodnight, I headed home out the back door.

I snuck into my grandmothers' room one last time before bed to give her a kiss on the cheek and say goodnight. I set the cake back on the kitchen table in waiting for my grandmother to wake and enjoy, then I tucked myself into bed on the couch and smiled at the thoughts of my day until I fell asleep.

I woke the next morning with one eye open, curious to see my grandmother moving around in the kitchen, excited to talk about the cake and night before, but the house was quiet. I slowly sat up, rubbing my eyes as I stood to my feet and began to fold up my blankets. I could see the piece of cake still sitting, untouched, on the kitchen table.

I made my way through the early part of the morning on my own, eating breakfast and cleaning up.

I snuck a couple of eggs and a piece of bread, mixed them up, and took them outside to feed Lucky. The grass was damp from a dew that had set through the night. There was a slight fog still in the air as the sun was yet to find its way into the day. As always, Lucky was excited to see me and as I approached he jumped up on me, scratching my bare chest as I balanced his bowl of food to keep from spilling over.

"Down, boy, Lucky, stay down," I yelped as I stepped back from his leaping body.

He calmed himself down after a few minutes of excitement and began to inhale his food.

The yard was calm; no Mr. Charlie or Hope or even Ms. Violet were to be seen. I sat beside Lucky until he finished his food and then I took the dish back to the house to wash up before my grandmother woke, if she hadn't already done so.

"Grandma, you gonna come eat 'chur cake?" I questioned loudly as I washed out Lucky's dish in the kitchen sink.

I dried the dish, put it away and went to see what she was doing.

As I stood in the frame of her bedroom door, she appeared to still be sleeping; she was still in the same position that I'd left her in the night before. I stood still, staring at her.

"Grandma!" I shouted hesitantly, and against my better judgment.

"Grandma, you gonna eat 'chur cake? We saved you a piece, we all thought we should save you a piece...thought you should have some too," I spoke loudly.

She didn't budge.

I walked the few feet next to her bedside, continuing to shout at her about the leftover piece of cake; still, she didn't move.

Standing next to her, as she laid under her blankets, I rested my head on her chest.

"Grandma, come eat 'chur cake, we lef' a piece jus for you, honest, we did, they all loved it…Hope, Ms. Violet and even Mr. Charlie, 'course he gonna eat two pieces, he loves his sweets, said it was delicious…grandma, come on, grandma, get up," I rambled on as I spoke softly against her chest.

I began to cry as I tugged on her arm, repeating myself over and over again about the cake.

Even though I wasn't completely familiar with death at that point something in me knew she wasn't going to wake up.

She was gone.

I continued to cry and ramble on about the piece of cake and my first birthday, until I tired myself out and fell asleep.

I woke up with the sun shining into her bedroom window as I found myself cuddled up next to her on her bed. The smell of her perfume filled the air.

I could hear Mr. Charlie outside, chopping wood, like he often did when he had the time to do so.

I climbed down off the bed and walked over to the window. I watched him chop wood for what seemed like forever, until I slowly made my way outside to be next to him.

He greeted me with cheer, as he always did, but I didn't say a word. With tears beginning to run down my cheeks I grabbed him by the hand and led him into the house to my grandmothers' bedside. He looked back at me as he gently wrapped his hand around her arm and then he slowly dropped his head.

"No need to make up no story, sir, I know she ain't gonna wake," I insisted softly.

"Have I ever lied to you, son?" he asked with care.

"No sir," I replied.

"Now you need to listen, and I know you ain't got much room to hear right now...but life ain't about what we lose, it ain't about what we think's been taken away, it's about what we gain from what we been given, from the time we had with somethin'," he explained as he looked down at me.

"Yes sir," I returned as I nervously clasped my hands together.

"Your grandma, she was a hard woman, real hard, she even whoop you at times...didn't she?" he spoke gently.

"Yes sir," I replied softly.

"But it was never without love. She even love you so much she gave you a birthday, jus last night, we all had some 'uh that cake she made for you. Now you ain't gotta be broke by this, jus as you ain't been broke by nothin' else in your short life. You got me and Ms. Violet, and now you got Hope, and we all on your side, no question," he went on with compassion as he kneeled down on one knee.

"Yes sir, thank you," I said with a slight smile, trying to see past the sadness.

"We gonna make this right," he suggested with care as he stood to his feet.

Mr. Charlie walked me over to his house, never taking his hand off my shoulder, and explained to Ms. Violet and Hope what had happened. He then said that he'd be back shortly and he left the house.

Ms. Violet wrapped her arms around me as tight as I'd ever felt a hug and held on to me until she slowly sat me down at the kitchen table. Hope was standing still with a look of unease on her face; she came and sat beside me.

"You okay?" Hope questioned with concern.

"I think so," I answered in short, smiling.

"You gonna have to move somewhere now?" she asked curiously.

"Nah, he ain't goin' nowhere, Sugar, don't 'chu worry 'bout that now," Ms. Violet spoke up.

I smiled gently at Ms. Violet as she winked back at me.

Hope sat with me at the kitchen table while Ms. Violet stayed busy cooking and baking for the day as we all visited with each other. They were both very kind with their effort to keep the mood light but everything still seemed to have an echo to it.

Mr. Charlie soon came back and he called me outside.

"I need you to go on into that forest there and I need you to pick out the prettiest tree you can find," he explained softly.

"Sir?" I asked, confused.

"You can take Sugar along if you want, and you go find yourself a tree, one you feel would be fit to lay your grandmother to rest in," he said with smile.

Even though I was having a hard time comprehending what he was saying, I knew he wasn't messing around. He was often called upon by people in the community to build the coffin when someone died; Mr. Charlie was a beautiful wood-maker.

I went back to the house and asked Hope if she'd join me. Ms. Violet spoke on her behalf and said *"she'd love to".* Hope smiled, stood up and came outside.

"We gonna take him?" Hope asked as she pointed at Lucky.

"May as well," I answered plainly.

"Okay," she replied.

"How am I 'posed to know which tree gonna suit her?" I asked of Mr. Charlie as we were walking away.

"You'll jus know, don't worry 'bout that none, you gonna know when you see it," he stated with confidence.

We wandered off into the forest, not saying too much, as Lucky ran off in front and disappeared.

"So jus what are we lookin' for?" Hope asked curiously.

"Need to find a tree to chop down to make a coffin for my grandma," I replied as I began to size up trees.

"You scared 'uh bein' alone now?" she asked, passing time.

"Nah, not really...been alone my whole life," I replied without thought.

"Well it ain't like you all by yourself anyway, you got me...I mean, you got us," she shyly suggested.

"Yeah, Mr. Charlie, he said the same thing," I said with a smile as I was staring up the long trunk of a tree.

Most of the trees were covered in moss up to about six feet from the ground and I didn't think Mr. Charlie was going to drag a stool out to the forest to stand on in order to chop it down, so we kept wandering around in search of the right tree.

Spending time with Hope seemed to calm the echoing in my mind; things weren't so hollow when she was near, she just had a way.

I got sick when I was a baby and almost died; I never remembered much of the illness but I do remember the face of this man who was always at my bedside. Most of the time he would just sit there watching over me or he'd hold my arm and softly sing to me. The words I could never remember but the tone of his voice I would never mistake if I heard it again. As I got older, I would ask my grandmother about him and who he was, but she insisted that I was making it up. She'd say *"you was so ill, child, you was probably jus imagining things."* I'd try to convince her that I was telling the truth but she tired easily and would just send me outside.

Hope gave me the same kind of comfort as that man had done when I was sick. It wasn't a feeling, and I didn't have to let myself go to any certain place to be at peace in her presence...I just was.

As we continued our way through the woods we could hear Lucky barking in the distance so we went in the direction of where it sounded like he was. Ducking our heads to get through some brush we came out in a small clearing at the foot of a tree where Lucky was sitting at, barking; even as he saw us, he didn't stop.

"What's 'ur problem?" Hope spoke to Lucky with a dry tone.

He just sat there, stopped barking for a moment, and then stood on all fours and began to kick away at the ground with his front paws.

As I was looking up and down at the tree in front of me I noticed there wasn't any moss on its base, as it stood on its own with just some small bushes and brush around it. Funny enough, it kind of resembled my grandmother; she surely wasn't near as tall as this old cedar was but strong and beautiful, and also kind of scary, well that, she certainly was.

"What he got?" Hope asked, tapping me on the arm to look at Lucky.

"How'd he get that?" I questioned as I pointed at him.

Lucky laid down on his stomach with his tongue hanging out, panting, while he had my old torn shirt, which I had buried in the river bank, stretched across his front paws.

"How the..." I said curiously, trying to get a grip on the moment.

"Ain't that somethin'," Hope insisted, laughing.

I pulled the shirt from Lucky's grip and stretched it out in front of me. I smiled thinking about the shaping of events over the last few days, and then as I thought of my grandmother I was quickly reminded that she was gone.

"So what now?" Hope asked, wisely interrupting my thoughts.

"Guess we go get Mr. Charlie 'n show him," I replied.

Hope and I, along with Lucky as he trailed behind, headed home to get Mr. Charlie.

When we got back home Mr. Charlie was outside by the shed sharpening his axe and saw, as he sat on his stump. I could smell Ms. Violet's cooking as it found its way into the early evening air through the kitchen window.

"You find what 'chu was lookin' for?" Mr. Charlie asked as he stopped working for a moment to light his pipe.

"Yes sir...might even say it found me," I answered with a proud sense of wonder.

"Well you best get in the house then and go eat...Ms. Violet been waiting on you two," he suggested, blowing his pipe smoke into the air.

"Yes sir," Hope and I spoke simultaneously.

Halfway through supper Mr. Charlie came in the house and sat down to eat. Ms. Violet insisted that I spend the night at their house and Mr. Charlie agreed without question. He said that he was going to head out in the morning to cut down the tree that I had picked out, stating that I should be ready to go along. Thankful for their love and concern, I agreed.

The four of us sat around the table eating and visiting with each other until late in the evening. Ms. Violet spent little time actually seated, as she continued to feed us with fresh baking and anything else she could fill us with. Hope kept trying to help her tidy up or encourage her to sit and enjoy some rest, but without any hesitation she declined and insisted that she needs no break. She didn't skip a beat as she floated around that little kitchen. Between words, serving food and cleaning up, she still found little moments to kiss me on the forehead or rub my back, without bringing any extra attention to me.

After we said goodnight to each other and I was tucked into a bed of blankets on the floor in the living room, I laid still with thoughts of my grandmother and the impending changes in my future without her presence.

Restlessly, I quietly got up and made my way outside. I managed to creep by Lucky without waking him on my way next door to my grandmothers' bedside.

She laid, seemingly peaceful, looking no different than she did when I went to wake her. I stood still next to her, mindlessly, without any words for minutes on end. The silence slowly began to interfere with me; I left the room and went back outside.

I quietly woke up Lucky, untied him, grabbed a lantern and Mr. Charlie's axe and went off into the woods. Lucky was still pretty tired as we trudged through the bushes, so he kept his distance behind me. Every few minutes he would let out a single bark to let me know where he was and I would call back to him to show my distance.

Arriving at the tree, which was soon to be my grandmothers' casket, I sized it up and down and wasted no time in attacking it with the freshly sharpened axe. Large chunks of rich smelling wood started to fly into the night air, hitting my bare chest and arms, filling my hair and landing all around me. I was increasingly angry with every swing; thoughts and feelings of a deep frustration flooded my body and mind as I beat that tree with every ounce of my being. From anger and hatred to tears and crying, then I was overcome with feelings of joy; I was filled with energy.

With the light of the moon and help from the lantern, as Lucky laid watching me, I wore that tree down until it teetered on its center; I was exhausted.

"Figured this where you was," a voice said as I felt a boot nudge me in the side, waking me up.

I opened my eyes to the sun shining down through the treetops; squinting, I rolled over to see the tall frame of Mr. Charlie standing over me.

"Mr. Charlie," I said, breathing inward.

"When'd you sneak off?" he asked, chuckling.

"Jus after I laid down…sorry, sir," I replied.

"You spend all night doin' that?" he questioned as he pointed at the tree with his axe.

"I think so…didn't even know I fell asleep," I returned, looking at the tree, only to see that it was still standing.

"You mus'a wiped yourself right out, boy," he suggested, smiling with pride.

"Guess so," I replied, rubbing my eyes.

I stood to my feet as he handed me the axe, gesturing toward the tree. I looked up the long trunk of that tree, closed my eyes for a moment as I thought of my grandmother and all of our struggles, and I began to swing the axe. I took a dozen or so swings with everything I had left in me and then Mr. Charlie grabbed me by the arm and pulled me back.

Everything went into slow motion as the tree began to fall. I could hear my breathing from within and my mind was empty in the most beautiful way. I could see each leaf as it parted from its limb on the crashing descent toward the ground. The whole world was opening up and showing itself to me inside of those very brief but stretched out seconds of life.

Mr. Charlie was using his hand to shade his eyes as he witnessed the tree fall; he was smiling, with what I would explain as a sense of pride, and he didn't blink until it hit a dead stop against the earth below.

"Ain't that sumthin'," he belted joyously.

I didn't say a word; I simply stood there, still as the morning air, and I smiled. Lucky didn't budge the entire time; he laid with his face on his front paws, staring at us.

Mr. Charlie smacked me on the back, nudging me forward as he smiled with excitement. He continued to rant about what a sight that just was and how proud of me he was. He said that Hope and Ms. Violet were worried about me when they saw that I had snuck out, but he explained to them that this was just something I needed to do, as a man.

"I told 'em, I knew you was out here and what you was up to. This jus how it is, how it's gotta be at times. You done right by your grandmother, and you done right by your future self. It's a good thing what you jus done, son, a real good thing," he explained as he began to sweep the branches from the trunk with quick, clean swipes of his axe.

"Yes sir," I replied as I started to snap branches off with my hands.

Mr. Charlie and I spent most of the morning in the woods, cleaning up the tree and scraping it clear of any branches or bark. As the day was getting increasingly hotter Hope came out to see us right around lunch time with some sandwiches and cold water. She didn't stay long or say too much, but she did give me heck for leaving in the middle of the night like I had done. I didn't mind though, nor did I say anything in my defense because she was so quick and hot headed it would've only made it worse; and Mr. Charlie sure thought it was all quite funny.

"Looks like you gettin' your lessons early, son," he said laughing as Hope walked away.

"Guess so," I said simply, shrugging my shoulders as I watched her leave with Lucky trailing behind.

He continued working away with his axe as I began to haul out what was going to be used to build the casket. Mr. Charlie had dragged his wood sleigh along with him when he came to find me that morning, which made it easier but still quite challenging to drag what we needed back out toward the house.

I was tired and sweat was steadily pouring out from my body but I didn't stop; I was determined to finish what I had started.

It was near suppertime when Mr. Charlie and I finished chopping and hauling out the wood from that big old tree and I was near death in energy but I felt like, more than ever before, I had what it took to be a man.

Ms. Violet was glowing with pride as the two of us walked in the house. Her and Hope spent most of the day together, baking and preparing supper for when we were all done.

We ate supper and shared stories of our days' events. Mr. Charlie poked fun at how Hope had lectured me but only he and Ms. Violet had a laugh about it. I wanted to laugh but Hope didn't so much as smile at the mention of it so I thought it would be better to let it be; I just continued eating as I listened.

After supper I washed up and put myself to bed on the floor, where I had escaped from the night before, while Mr. Charlie and Ms. Violet sat visiting in the kitchen just feet away.

Hope sat nearby on a chair and we talked, about nothing in particular, until I fell asleep. I did my best to stay awake for as long as I could to enjoy her company but it was short lived.

I woke up the next morning to Mr. Charlie heading outside; I knew there was still work to be done so I was up and right there behind him.

The day was spent with Mr. Charlie teaching me how to build a casket for my grandmother. I had my hands in wherever I could, and it was encouraged. He explained to me that building the casket, from beginning to end, would be a good outlet to part ways with any anger or negative energy that I may still have toward her; stating that the process could be used to release her spirit and find peace within mine.

He always spoke so purposeful and for the most part I understood what he was saying but more than anything I liked listening to him talk. When he told stories or spoke on his philosophies there was always a very simple but, kind and limber, and beautiful truth to his words. Ms. Violet said that he had the soul of a lion and the tongue of a weathered slave. Her label alone of him was enough to keep me listening when he spoke.

Hope and Ms. Violet came outside throughout the day to visit and bring us food and water. There wasn't a lot of time to take breaks because my grandmother was still in need of her final resting place, and with the heat like it was our time to complete her burial was that much more important. The sun was beating down with the same fierce intention as the day before, so we were both dripping with sweat once again.

When the casket was near complete, Mr. Charlie set me up to finish it and then I was to use an old rag to saturate the wood with linseed oil to help protect it from rotting. After I was done with that I was to go meet him at the church to help him dig the grave.

Everything was happening so fast since my grandmother died and I was so busy and determined that I didn't have much interest in thinking outside of the task at hand. I know she wouldn't want many wasted thoughts on her behalf anyway, and as I saw it, I'd have a lifetime to reflect if need be.

It was starting to get late by the time I made my way to the church so I brought Lucky and Hope along for some company during the walk. We didn't speak all that much but our bond was growing stronger with each moment that we shared, so it was nice just to have her by my side. I had my shovel dragging behind me in one hand as I held a jug of water in the other.

Ms. Violet, showing some concern, sent me off with a rag wrapped around my neck, which she'd soaked in cold water to keep me cool as the evening air wasn't dropping in temperature.

As we arrived at the church, with Lucky trailing behind, Mr. Charlie was already down past his knees into the earth.

"Where you leave *your* shovel, little Miss Hope?" he asked of her as he looked up at us, smiling with delight.

"I ain't bring no shovel, he jus told me to come along," she replied shyly as she pointed at me.

"You figure there gonna be enough room for the both of us in here, without you smackin' me with your shovel or fillin' my boots with dirt?" Mr. Charlie asked with joy as he looked at me, then down at the hole in which he stood.

"Think so, sir, should be jus fine; you keep outta my way and I'll keep outta your boots," I returned, smiling.

Hope stood next to Lucky, giggling, as they watched me find room for myself next to Mr. Charlie in the hole.

We dug down into the ground where my grandmother would forever rest, while we exchanged banter in a very playful and loving tone. Hope circled us continuously in an effort to not miss anything; she counted his scoops and then mine, out loud, as we played back and forth over which one of us was doing most of the digging. With the sun setting behind the trees, Hope lit up the lantern and set it down on the ground beside the hole.

Before I knew it we had dug so deep that I couldn't see anything but the silhouette of Hope as she stood in the glow of the lantern. Mr. Charlie hoisted me up onto the grass and then spent a short time longer shoveling. Hope and I sat down, dangling our feet into the hole below, and with Lucky in between us we watched as Mr. Charlie squared off each corner and leveled the bottom to what was as close to perfection as possible.

He spoke to us about life and how precious it was. He insisted on the importance of not becoming hateful or angry because of things that happen to us along the way. He talked a lot about love and having faith in a persons' heart, even when their actions may blur our vision. Mr. Charlie, calmly, all from the darkness of a freshly dug grave, lightened the weight of my heart as I sat next to my best friend.

The three of us, and Lucky, slowly made our way home in the dark shadows of the tall roadside trees as I held the lantern at my side while Hope continued to walk into it with her limp. I didn't bother switching hands to hold it because it was just such a great little moment each time it happened.

The next morning when I woke up, the house was empty. I folded up my blankets and went to the back door to have a look outside; no one was to be seen. I sat down at the kitchen table and I didn't move for a few minutes as I stayed in wonder about where everyone was. Shortly after, Ms. Violet and Hope came into the house.

"Mornin', sweetheart, you sleep well?" Ms. Violet asked with love in her tone.

"Yes ma'am, slept right through," I answered softly.

"Okay, baby, we gotta get you dressed and ready for church," she explained as she rubbed my back.

"Yes ma'am," I replied, looking at Hope.

Hope handed me a bundle of folded clothes and Ms. Violet instructed me to go wash up and change into them. I didn't so much as ask where they came from, I just did as I was told.

When I was all done and dressed I walked out into the kitchen just as I could hear singing coming from outside. Ms. Violet and Hope were waiting for me as they had also changed their clothes; one was wearing a black dress while the other was wearing a bright yellow dress with a pattern of tiny flowers on each cuff of its high sleeves; I smiled at the sight of her as she stood quietly, waiting.

Ms. Violet led me by the hand outside, into the backyard. There must have been fifty people singing as they stood around the casket of my grandmother. It was placed carefully on an old wooden carrier, sitting in the shade of the tree that stretched out over the garden. Ms. Violet gently held my hand and walked with me next to the casket. I looked back to see Hope following slowly on our heels. The singing slowed to a steady humming of beautiful sounds as people rubbed my back and softly patted me on the head with love. The faces were all familiar from church and each one of them had a glowing smile of kindness on it.

Mr. Charlie initiated the funeral procession as he and three other men picked up the wooden carrier and began to walk. Ms. Violet, Hope and I, were close behind while everyone else walked along-side and behind us as the humming transformed, in sync, back into singing.

Ms. Violet didn't let go of my hand for the entire walk, nor did Mr. Charlie or anyone else so much as pause for a break. The sun continued to break briefly behind the clouds which was a great gift as it was already quite hot out. Hope kept up, continuously looking over at me and smiling just enough to greet me. None of it was comfortable for me but everyone was doing such a beautiful service of kindness that it created an ease within me.

Walking up the grass through the churchyard to the back where the grave was dug, I started to get butterflies in my stomach. As we approached the grave, Hope came around the backside of Ms. Violet and held my other hand; my nerves immediately settled.

The casket was set down and the top was removed so anyone who wished could have their final goodbye in person, so to speak. People slowly made their way past my grandmother and briefly stared at her, while some whispered a few parting words. I watched from a short distance, but didn't walk past the casket; I had my time with her at her bedside and that was enough for me.

Slowly, the casket was lowered into the ground as the singing began. I didn't see one person crying, nor did I shed a single tear. The energy and the way in which people responded to her last day upon the surface of earth was very fitting to who she was and how she spent her time, just as it was; any sadness had simply passed on with her departure.

The majority of the dirt was shoveled back into the hole, covering my grandmother as she lay in her casket, and then Mr. Charlie walked over as everyone was still saying goodbye in song, and he handed me a shovel.

The few minutes after that was the only part of the day that I don't quite remember.

CHAPTER 7

Over the next few days I spent most of my time going through my grandmothers' belongings, as I did my best to find my place among her small home by myself. For as long as I could remember she dictated the energy in the house and my place of belonging among her was always in question.

Each night after she died I told myself to sleep in her bed but out of habit and fear of her catching me, from beyond even death itself, I continued to spend my hours dreaming on the couch where I had done so since the beginning.

Hope stayed with me during the day and into the evening whenever I wasn't at her house or when we weren't messing around outside; and with my grandmother being gone, I started to keep Lucky in the house with me through the night, which kept me company.

I took some of my grandmothers' clothes and smaller items that would never be of any use to me down to the church and left them there for those that may need any of it. Hope helped me in any way that she could. I did, however, keep my grandmothers' perfume and I found myself lightly spraying the air within the house for a sense of comfort as I needed it.

Ms. Violet and Mr. Charlie were very supportive of me living by myself, even though at first they did their best to convince me to live with them until I was further prepared to be on my own. Even as the days went by Ms. Violet would remind me that their door was always open if I came to change my mind.

I worked the garden every day, picking weeds and hauling water to it whenever it didn't get rain. Hope, as always, was by my side along with Lucky, helping or just keeping me company as I found my days becoming more frequented by chores and little projects around the house.

Mr. Charlie gave me some paint that he had taken from work when they were cleaning out one of the old shops which was being rebuilt after it caught fire and had burnt half the building to the ground.

"Why you wanna paint these?" Hope asked as she helped me prepare the paint.

"They jus old, and I think they need a change...don't you?" I replied, speaking of the kitchen cupboards.

"Yeah, I guess so, but we ain't even got enough 'uh one color to do the whole thing," she said with concern.

None of the paint cans were full; they each had half or less than half and none were of the same color.

"That don't matter none, we'll jus do what we can," I returned, smiling, as I stirred up the first can.

With some rags that I'd made, by way of cutting up some of my grandmothers' "good linen", as she would have called it, Hope and I began to paint the cupboards above the kitchen counter. For as small as the kitchen was it sure seemed to have a lot of cupboard space.

As we finished one can I would stir up the next, and one after another, we painted and laughed and dreamed out loud with each other, side by side; all without any limit on how loud or messy or childish we could be. It was something that I was quickly becoming accustomed to and very much enjoying.

"You was right, it did jus need a change 'uh look in here," Hope said as she stepped back to look at the newly painted kitchen cup-boards.

As each cupboard door was a mixture of different colors and all the paint was gone, the house that had never felt like mine was slowly beginning to feel like a place where I belonged.

Hope and I stood next to each other, smiling at our combined efforts in claiming that space with an all but professional paint job, as we started to laugh.

With my hand lightly brushing against hers as we stood next to each other laughing, we both stopped instantly in the awkward realization of the moment. I looked down at my hand just as she was doing to hers and simultaneously we dropped the paint soaked rags from our opposite hands.

I quickly bent over to pick them up but I was still not fast enough; they had already left a glob of paint where each of them had fallen from our grips.

"You wanna clean rag to mop that up?" Hope questioned, sounding startled from the moment before.

"I think it'll jus smear...maybe I can scrape it up after it dry some," I answered, looking down at the floor.

For all of the time that we had spent together and the increasing strength in our friendship by each passing day, there was suddenly a very strange feeling stirring within me after that single awkward moment occurred.

Silently, we both began to clean up the paint cans and rags that we had scattered to catch any drips from our painting.

Hope went home for supper and I stayed behind, mostly just to try and slow my mind and calm my nerves. I laid down on the couch with Lucky on the floor next to me and with my stomach in knots I surrendered, and just smiled to myself in wonder.

Later that evening Ms. Violet came over with a plate of food made up for me.

"Well, well, well, ain't you jus a little man; look at what 'chu done in here, sweetheart, good for you, it looks beautiful, *jus beautiful!*" she exclaimed as she looked around, noticing the fresh paint and changes that were made within the small space.

"Thank you, ma'am," I replied with a big smile, proud to hear her words.

"I brought you some dinner, baby. Why didn't you come with Sugar, you know you always welcome at our table...it's as good as your very own," she spoke with love as she set the plate down on the table, taking the cover off.

"I know, ma'am, thank you, I was jus havin' a rest is all," I said as I sat down at the table.

"Well listen to you, darlin', ain't you jus turnin' into a fine young man...and quick as the wind you growin' up," she insisted with pride as she set a fork and knife down in front of me, kissing me on the forehead.

"Ain't got much choice now, Ms. Violet," I replied as I looked around the kitchen.

"You always got a choice, sweetheart, and you makin' all the right ones far as I can tell. I jus wanna let you know how proud 'uh you I am...how proud we all are. You doin' a real fine job with what you been given, and I know it ain't been easy for you, but times'll change and you gonna be alright...you well on your way," she explained with love as she smiled, watching me eat.

"Thank you, ma'am, you and Mr. Charlie...you been such a big part 'uh anything that's good in me, and I ain't never gonna be able to repay you for all that you done. Now Hope come along and she the first friend I ever had, so I jus ain't got nothin' to be down about, I got nothin' but warmth 'n goodness all around me," I said in return as I felt a sense of pride for my life.

"Sweetie, you ain't never got nothin' to repay us for, we love you as though you been our own child from our first introduction. You been jus as special for us, Poor Boy, and it's a gift jus to watch you grow," she explained, not once looking away from me as she held onto my hand.

"Thank you, ma'am, I love you jus the same...with all my heart," I said in short.

Ms. Violet had a way about her that always kept me at ease; when she spoke you just knew that she meant what she was saying and it was always without any conditions. Her love was the truth and her words were perfect to match.

The two of us sat and visited while I finished eating, then she and I washed and dried the plate she'd brought as well as some left over dirty dishes I had in the sink. She spent some time with me around the house making sure I knew how to wipe everything down properly and keep a clean living space. My grandmother never let me get away with keeping or making a mess in the house, so I was well aware of all that Ms. Violet was showing me but I didn't want to ruin the moment as she was so kind and encouraging with her efforts; plus, I thoroughly enjoyed spending time with her, regardless of what we were doing.

A short time later, Hope came knocking at the back door with a piece of pie for me.

"You ain't gotta knock, you welcome here anytime you wish to come," I snickered as I opened the screen door for her.

"I was told to come bring you some pie and to see what all the fuss about," she said as she put the pie down on the table.

"He ain't foolin' nobody, he jus lookin' for a moment to his'self," Ms. Violet spoke up, laughing, thinking out loud about Mr. Charlie.

"Yeah, I kinda figured that so I jus did as he asked," Hope replied, beginning to laugh.

The three of us shared in a good laugh about Mr. Charlie and his funny ways, each with a great appreciation for his heart and his humor.

Hope stayed behind when Ms. Violet left after she said that she'd given Mr. Charlie enough time to disrupt her house; as she left she had a laugh, saying that she was *"gonna go give that old rascal a scare".*

"You want some pie, Hope?" I asked as I grabbed a fork from the drawer.

"Brought that for you," she answered as she stood with her hands together in front her.

"I don't mind to share," I insisted as I grabbed a second fork and sat down at the table.

She slowly made her way across the kitchen floor to the table and sat down. We shared the piece of pie as we laughed and joked about Ms. Violet and Mr. Charlie.

Lucky laid at our feet next to the table, smelling like he'd been bathing in hot trash. The two of us started laughing hysterically as we caught wind of his smell, then he looked up at us with this look of pathetic desperation, as though he already knew how awful he smelled.

"We gotta give him a bath...he smell like he been diggin' around in Mr. Charlie's fish bucket," I suggested, laughing, as I slid back on my chair to stand up.

"Where we gonna wash him?" Hope asked curiously, looking around.

"The tub, I guess...I'll jus put some water to boil," I replied as I began to fill the pot we used for boiling water.

Hope ran some cold water to fill the bottom of the tub while we waited for the pot on the stove to reach a boil.

With his demeanor still seemingly embarrassed, Lucky had made his way under the kitchen table against the wall. Hope was standing back, gently lecturing him, trying to coax him out from hiding; he didn't budge.

I carried the pot into the bathroom, dumped it into the tub and then waited a few minutes for the water to mix and cool just slightly.

I called Lucky's name from the bathroom and without hesitation I heard his nails scramble across the floor as he ran toward my voice.

"Oh ain't that a big surprise," Hope belted, expressing her annoyance for Lucky as she followed right behind him.

As soon as he reached my side I picked him up and put him in the tub; he loved it. He dropped down to his belly and began to roll around as he found the room to do so. Hope and I laughed as he splashed around, quickly soaking the floor at the tubs' side.

After he settled down we managed to keep him calm enough to give him a good scrubbing with some of my grandmothers' soap, and then a rinse with clean water from the tap as all of his filth was finding its way down the drain. We used my grandmothers' towel to dry him off as best as we could before he took off running laps around the house with excitement. As he was ducking and dodging furniture and sliding into walls, Hope and I were laughing so hard that I slipped on the wet floor trying to keep up with him, which only increased the volume of our laughter.

It wasn't long after that Mr. Charlie was at the back door to walk Hope home, leaving Lucky and I to tuck ourselves into bed, with me on the couch and him at my side on the floor. I spoke lightly to him, about nothing in particular, until my speech slowed and I fell asleep.

The next week or so was much of the same; some garden work, some play time with Hope and Lucky and lots of visiting with Mr. Charlie and Ms. Violet. They were very adamant in keeping a strong role in my daily life and learning, both teaching me different ways of growing into a young man but also making sure that I knew the importance of being a boy and enjoying myself in all that I did.

Chapter 8

Weeks had passed since my grandmothers' death and life was moving along just fine. Mr. Charlie found room for me to make some money with him at work; it wasn't much but it gave me a chance to make a little something for myself and Ms. Violet said she would help me manage some savings if that was something I wanted to do; she was such a smart woman.

I didn't go to work until close to evening time when everyone else was finishing up for the day because it was my job to clean up where need be for the following day. Hope and Ms. Violet would either meet me at my house with some warm supper and we'd visit and laugh into the night or I'd just go straight over to their house after work and eat there.

Lucky walked with me to work and he'd go off snooping around or just patiently wait for me to finish. My boss, Mr. Nelson, seemed to really like Lucky and he'd always have an old soup bone or something for him when we arrived and then he'd leave shortly after. He was really happy with my efforts and would leave with the same words each day that I worked…*"You keep doin' what you been doin' 'round here, the way you been doin' it, and you gonna find your-self tellin' gown men what to do in no time".* The first few times I heard him say it, it was a lot to keep up with because he spoke so quickly, but eventually I caught up with his words and I'd just smile and say, "Yes sir, thank you, sir", then he'd go on his way and I'd continue working.

I always did more than I was told or left with to do and I always worked as fast as I could to get it done. I liked working and I enjoyed knowing that I was earning my own money, however little it was, so it was always important for me to do my best each time I was there and I didn't want to let Mr. Charlie down; after all, I was there because of him.

One evening when I was at work and everybody had gone their way for the day, Lucky wandered off into one of the shops out back that was used mostly just for storage. I wouldn't have even known he found his way back there had he not spent so much time barking that I couldn't help but seek him out.

The sun was finding its way behind the tall trees that surrounded the back side of the property, so the front of each building on that tree line had succumb to the shadows of rooftops. I couldn't see Lucky and he wasn't coming to me as I called him but his barking didn't slow for even a second; however, he didn't sound threatened, he sounded like he'd found something.

As I made my way into the back of the building, through the fading light, I followed the sound of his bark to the bottom of some stairs that led up and into a room above the shop. I called out his name four or five more times from the bottom of the stairs as I stood still, but he was making it quite clear that he wouldn't stop until I was at his side. Slowly, I made my way up the stairs beginning to find myself annoyed with Lucky, and a little scared with what I would find as the source of his incessant barking. I continued to call his name as I took each step, then once I made it to the top I quit speaking and stood still for a moment, before turning the corner to reach his now near sounding bark. I pivoted on my back leg as I slowly turned into the doorway of the room which was overlooking the shop floor. Just as I poked my head around the corner I immediately saw Lucky, and before I could even blink, my eyes scrolled up and found their way into the eyes of a tall, broad shouldered man who stood still at the foot of Lucky. I froze for a few seconds and then as Lucky turned his head to see me, the man took a step forward in my direction and I took three, big, quick steps back. On my third step back, the last thing I remember is there being no surface under my right foot; then everything went black.

"You okay son?" a strange voice asked as I slowly opened my eyes.

I was lying down in the room above the shop where I had fallen from; it was dimly lit by the flickering of a burning lantern and a man appeared before me, sitting in a chair at my side.

"Yes sir, I think so," I answered hesitantly.

"Don't worry, boy, I'm not gonna bring you no harm," he insisted with concern as he patted me softly on my chest.

"What happened?" I asked as I slowly sat up, leaning back on my elbows.

"You took a fall; it wasn't more than some luck that you landed on that old pile of tires down there...and maybe if you wasn't so startled by seeing me you wouldn't have had your lights go out," he explained softly.

"Where's my dog?" I asked as I scanned the room for Lucky.

"He's there, in the corner. After he was done shouting at me we made acquaintances, then he watched and made sure it wasn't my intention to harm you," he replied, smiling, as he looked over at Lucky who was tucked into the corner on an old blanket.

"How long I been here?" I questioned him.

"A couple of hours, can't see no more than that," he replied as he stood to his feet.

He was a large man, tall with broad shoulders, but a slender frame; he had a beard, and from what I could see his hair looked kind of shaggy and unattended to. When he spoke, it sounded different from what I had grown used to; it wasn't as lazy as what I'd been accustomed to hearing.

"What's your name, son?" he asked as he walked across the room.

"My name?" I questioned. "Poor Boy, sir, my name's, Poor Boy," I replied slowly.

"Poor Boy, huh…how'd you get yourself a name like that?" he asked curiously.

"Jus sorta stuck I guess; didn't have no name when my mom gave me up and my grandmother didn't bother to gimme no real name, so that's jus what I been called," I explained as he listened carefully.

"I like that, that sounds just fine to me," he said as he smiled and winked at me with a very gentle glisten.

"You got yourself a proper name, sir?" I asked as I slowly stood to my feet.

"Well, I ain't got too many people who call on me, but those that do…they call me, Prophet," he replied with a proud but somewhat lonely sounding tone.

He grabbed the lantern and swung it in the grips of his large hand to shine the light on Lucky, who was still sound asleep in the corner on the floor. As the light drifted through the room across the floor, I caught a glance at his feet in my quick survey of him; they were the biggest feet I'd ever seen and were without the covering of any shoes.

"You ain't got no shoes on, mister," I blurted out before I could stop myself from speaking.

"*Don't I know it!* Truth is, I haven't had a pair 'uh shoes on these feet for as long as I been walking," he said without hesitation.

"Why's that, sir?" I asked curiously.

"I like to feel the earth under my toes…it keeps me close to God," he replied, smiling as he nodded, patting his hand against his chest.

"I ain't never heard nobody with no shoes, hidin' out in another mans' shop, be sayin' he close to God," I spoke without caution.

"You work around here?" he asked, looking out the dusty window into the night.

"Yes, sir, I work here...for Mr. Nelson," I replied, staring at him as I stood still.

"I ain't never seen no boy wearing a Sunday shirt, missing all but three buttons, tearing it up at work like he don't give a damn," he said in return with a dry tone.

After my grandmother died I was able to wear whatever I chose for the day and most days I didn't wear a shirt at all, especially when it was so hot out, until it was time to go to work. But when I went to work I'd put on my "Sunday shirt", which most people would refer to as their church clothes or "Sundays' best". In this case though, I'd torn most of the buttons off of it snagging it on things as I was working, so I just kept wearing it that way.

"It's all I got, sir," I said simply as I looked down at my bare belly poking through the opening of my shirt.

That was the first time I ever had someone put me in my place without making me feel like I was worthless. All he did was talk to me the way I had done to him, out of judgment, but it was gentle and point proving, not mean. I slowly bowed my head and smiled softly to myself as I felt a fresh sense of curiosity within.

We continued our little back and forth for a short while, not getting into anything too personal or intrusive, just light conversation about my work at the mill and such things.

Once Lucky woke up and stood to his feet, after stretching his body across the floor, he made his way to my side and shortly after saying a goodbye we started on our journey home. Uncertain if I would see my new friend Prophet again, I shook his hand in thanks for our time together and his looking out for me after my fall.

When I got home Mr. Charlie was outside, chopping wood. The sun was just finding its place in the early morning sky and there was a light dew that had set through the quick, passing night. I could hear the smacking of his axe against the wood as I was coming up to the front of the house. I was feeling slightly nervous about him seeing me just getting home because I didn't want him to worry about what happened to me at work, and I wasn't sure how to explain to him about the strange man hiding out in the shop.

I would have gone in through the front door of the house, and avoided him all together, but my grandmother had a large shelf up against it and kept it locked so no one would use it. So instead, I waited patiently, keeping Lucky close to me and quiet, until I heard Mr. Charlie go inside his house and then I went into mine, un-detected.

I took my shirt off and threw it over the kitchen chair just as I noticed a plate of food sitting on the table with a fork and a glass of water beside it.

"Look at how blessed I am, boy, look at that...they feed me even when I'm nowhere in sight," I said to Lucky as I unwrapped the plate and sat down to eat.

I ate almost everything on the plate and I what I didn't eat I scraped into Lucky's dish by the backdoor, but he appeared to be as tired as I was. He walked over to his dish and looked at it for a few moments then followed me into the next room and laid on the floor at my side as I tucked myself in, on the couch.

"Poor Boy, you in there, you home?" Ms. Violet spoke out as she opened the back door, waking me up.

"Yes ma'am, I'm here," I replied as I laid on the couch, feeling sleepless.

"Where you been, child?...half the day come and gone and we ain't even laid eyes on you," she said with concern.

"I know, ma'am, I'm sorry...I didn't mean nothin' by it, jus tired is all," I replied slowly as I sat up.

"You feelin' alright, you sick?" she asked as she put her hand on my forehead.

"Yes ma'am, I feel fine, jus tired," I answered, squinting with one eye closed.

"I see you ate your dinner," she said as she sat down beside me, smiling.

"Yes ma'am, thank you," I replied with a smile.

"That was Sugar who lef' that for you; she insisted on bringin' you some food but said you wasn't home," Ms. Violet said as she patted me on the leg then stood to her feet and walked into the kitchen.

"I was at the mill pretty late," I explained in short.

I did my best to change the subject and not talk about work, which with Ms. Violet was easy because she got busy tidying up, as she always did, and wasn't completely listening to me. Although she was great at multitasking, when cleaning or cooking, and being able to carry on a conversation, I learned long ago that if she caught something important or pressing enough she would stop what she was doing in order to communicate; otherwise, she just kind of floated through chitchat with one ear.

That afternoon, Hope and I went for a walk into the woods out back, with Lucky trailing behind. We made our way to the creek as the sun was beating down with such might that even the still air was hot.

Hope asked me where I was the night before, seemingly curious, but I stumbled around it just as I had done with Ms. Violet, managing to not say anything too in depth. I wanted to tell her, I wanted to share the whole night with her but I didn't know how she'd respond and I certainly didn't want her grandparents to find out. I told myself I'd give it a few days and then I'd say something if I needed to let it out.

We hung out and laughed, sharing small and big dreams with each other, like we did with most of our time together. Hope stayed close to the waters' edge while Lucky and I splashed around in a calm, shallow pool nearby. My caution and fear of the water seemed to get neglected when Hope was around.

My dreams, as I spoke of them, consisted mostly of working and making a living for myself; although money wasn't something that had ever been a part of my life. In fact, the palm of my hand had never held a single coin, and now with where I was, essentially alone, money was becoming my relation to freedom.

Hope was much different with the picture she had for her future; money was never mentioned, not once. She spoke a lot about wanting to be a ballerina or work with sick animals. Both of which were great dreams, beautiful dreams, but between her leg and her seeming lack of connection with Lucky, it was hard for me to see it as anything but a dream. Although the way she spoke of each was with such a determined tone, it was tough not to believe her or believe in her. It was as though her future was simply waiting for her arrival, in whatever form she showed up.

Her attitude most of the time was that of a stubborn old woman, although she was very much a girly girl but also really had no inhibitions about getting dirty. She was remarkable, inside and out, and I always, wholeheartedly, enjoyed every minute we shared together.

That evening, on my walk to work I was anxious about whether or not I'd see Prophet again, or if I'd be confronted by Mr. Nelson in regards to the matter.

I used Lucky as a buffer when I first showed up and Mr. Nelson greeted us at the gate. I talked briefly about our time at the creek and did my best to keep the topic of conversation off of work, aside from my evening duties; plus, he was always happy to see Lucky which made for an easy distraction. Lucky reminded him of a dog he had when he was *"'bout the same size"*, as he put it, when he directed his index finger into my chest, speaking of me in comparison.

Mr. Nelson parted as he always did, with a quick few words of wisdom and an old bone for Lucky, leaving me to get busy working.

Soon after he left I made my way to the back shop where I last saw Prophet, the night before. With the sun still above the trees there was a lot of light being cast in through the windows on the back wall, which made everything look a lot different than I remembered it to be. As I called out for Prophet and made my way up the stairs, the air was still; no sounds or sights to question and no Prophet to be seen. When I found myself in the room over the shop where I woke the night before, after falling, it appeared untouched; for how long I couldn't tell but it definitely hadn't seen any organizing or even a broom in years. I wasn't able to walk freely for three feet before running into something, whereas the night before the room was essentially clear of anything. I was getting confused about what happened or how it could be that things changed so drastically and so fast. I walked out onto the landing where I had fallen from and it had a railing across it, which I couldn't remember from the night before and which also would have prevented my fall. I looked over the railing toward the shop floor, only to see a stack of rusty steel in the box of an old pick-up truck, which was covered in dust and looked like it hadn't moved in years and most certainly would have left me in very poor condition had that been what I landed on.

I sat down on the stairs as I tried to make sense of everything. Lucky found his way to me and then sat down beside me after he took inventory of his surroundings.

"This don't seem right, does it?" I spoke out, looking at Lucky as he stared at me with his panting tongue hanging out.

After a few minutes of confusion and trying to clear my head I stood up and made my way downstairs to get back to work. As I passed the old truck filled with scrap metal I ran my finger across the hood through its thick layer of dust, as I shook the last of my wonder about the events from the night before.

I finished up my work for the day and chained then locked the gate to the yard on my way out, like always, and headed home.

It was a warm summer evening and the road home was very dusty. There wasn't a lot of vehicle traffic closer to where I lived but when there was, Lucky and I had to turn our backs' to the road and wait for the dust to settle, which left us standing still at times for several minutes. There were steep ditches on either side of the road as well so it would get interesting trying to find your way back on a straight path as the sun was going down. Most people would slow down and didn't kick up much dust but every so often some *'young fool'*, as Mr. Charlie would call them, would drive by with a heavy foot and pay no mind to people walking.

When I got home Hope and Mr. Charlie were out back, in the garden. Lucky slowly made his way to say hello and I washed the dust from my face in the barrel beside the house.

"All done?" Mr. Charlie asked of me from across the yard as I splashed water on my face.

"Yes sir, all done for today," I replied, patting my face dry with my shirt.

"Atta be, son, good, good to hear!" he exclaimed as he stood up straight, leaning on the end of his hoe.

Ms. Violet called me into the house from the kitchen window. She sat me down with a plate of food that she had ready for me, and directed me to eat. Whenever I sat down with them and we all ate together, she or Mr. Charlie would say grace, but if I was eating alone she would never force me to say grace or anything else. I caught her a few times whispering *'thank you lord'* to herself as she served me but she never once forced me to say anything on my own.

The two of us visited while I ate and she cleaned up around the kitchen. Every chance she had she would let me know that they could always make room for me at their house, and that I didn't have to be all alone where I was. And each time I would remind her that I had Lucky to keep me company and that I was always okay, especially in knowing that she was just next door. She was concerned, naturally, and it felt good to know how much she cared but I really was beginning to enjoy having my own space.

Whenever we had some time to ourselves Ms. Violet would sit down with me and have me spell out different words and then use them in a sentence with the proper pronunciation. The way that I spoke, for the most part, was just out of habit and laziness but Ms. Violet was sure adamant about me, as well as Hope, being able to function anywhere, beyond how we may appear to others. She would say, *"You can fool 'em with your looks, but once you open your mouth, that's all on you, and you can't hide from that".*

We practiced for a short time until Mr. Charlie and Hope came in from outside. Ms. Violet told them to go wash up then we all sat down and had some freshly baked pie, hot out of the oven, and a cold glass of milk.

As we did most nights, we stayed up visiting and laughing around the kitchen table, listening to Mr. Charlie tell his stories while Ms. Violet would smile and correct him on parts, or fling her towel at him and call him a fool, then she'd kiss him on the side of his head. It was a small space, but it was sure filled with a lot of love.

The next morning, I woke up to Hope standing at my side as I laid on the couch; she stood over me, calling my name. As I opened my eyes I saw her holding a plate of food in one hand and a fish hook in the other.

"C'mon, get up, we goin' fishin'," she demanded with a dry tone.

"Huh?" I replied in a daze.

"Get up!" she instructed me.

I did just as she said.

It had been a while since I went fishing, and I'm not sure how it came about, but after I ate the breakfast she'd brought me we went outside to where Mr. Charlie waited on us with his steel bucket and rod, and off we went.

There was a thick fog in the early morning air as we stayed tight on the heels of Mr. Charlie, through the forest, toward his claimed fishing hole; it was a place that he and I used to frequent but hadn't visited in some time. We would plan trips the night before so we could get a couple of hours in prior to him going to work. This was the first time Hope came along and Mr. Charlie was quite proud to speak of our times shared together as we walked along.

Lucky was being lazy and was too tired to get up so he stayed behind.

"We best pick it up if we gonna catch anything before the sun gets too high," Mr. Charlie spoke out, encouraging a faster pace.

We were only able to fish from one side and once the sun came up it would cast our shadows onto the water which wasn't any good for fishing because it would deter the fish from biting.

"Yes sir," Hope and I spoke simultaneously as we picked up our pace side by side.

"He sure pushy 'bout this...it's that good?" Hope asked, struggling to keep up, swinging her stiff leg over deadfall as I kept the pace next to her.

"You can count on it...ain't that right, Poor Boy? Go on, Sugar, jus ask him, he'll tell you!" Mr. Charlie exclaimed from nearly ten feet in front of us.

"It's true, Mr. Charlie speakin' the truth...'specially when it comes to the fishin' hole," I said proudly in return.

"We gonna see about this, the fishin' won't lie," Hope responded as she was falling short of breath.

"Last one to catch a fish, cleans 'em all!" Mr. Charlie shouted as we arrived at the waters' edge.

The three of us scrambled to get our hooks in the water after we positioned ourselves in what we each thought was the perfect spot. Laughing and stumbling around, I had my hook in the water first, then Hope, and then just seconds after was Mr. Charlie. As the fog was lifting and the early morning air was warming up, the water looked like it was steaming and you could see the mouths of fish come to the surface, grab a bug and then go back under. Caught up in the excitement of being the first to catch a fish, and having little experience, Hope kept pulling her hook out and quickly tossing it back into the direction of where a fish had just surfaced. I laughed, which she scolded me for, while Mr. Charlie was set into his flow.

"Uh ohhh...down to you two now," I shouted as I pulled my first fish out of the water.

No more than a single minute went by and Mr. Charlie pulled a fish out, hanging from his hook.

"Shhhuuuggarrr!" Mr. Charlie yelled as it echoed off the surrounding trees.

"This stinks, I ain't never cleaned a fish in my life," Hope shouted as she threw her wooden rod to the ground.

"Hey now...." Mr. Charlie returned as he laughed.

Hope sat down on a nearby tree stump, glaring at me as I laughed.

"It ain't my fault you had your hook in the air more than the water," I said, shrugging my shoulders as I stood to throw my hook back in.

"Atta boy, son, see how far that gets you," Mr. Charlie spoke out, laughing, as he continued to fish.

Hope stayed positioned on her tree stump as Mr. Charlie and I kept fishing. One after another, we continued to pull fish out of the water as Hope rolled her eyes and grumbled about how we were just trying to make more work for her, but we just laughed in enjoyment of the morning.

Mr. Charlie had this lightness about him where very few things ever got to him. He found humor in almost every situation, and that was something I was learning to do as well. Hope's behavior wasn't anything more than just frustration so we were all very playful about it.

After we filled the bucket and it neared time for Mr. Charlie to get to work, we headed home.

Lucky found his way out to us as we were near halfway back in the direction toward home. With Hope making little effort to crawl out of her mood, seeing Lucky proved to be an immediate change in her behavior. Mr. Charlie and I kept walking while Hope and Lucky greeted each other and played for a few minutes.

"She sure stubborn, ain't she?" I suggested to Mr. Charlie as we walked.

"That's a good thing, son, she gonna need that," he replied, looking back at her.

"Sir?" I asked curiously.

"The world ain't gonna be easy on her, so that heat, that fire she's got, it's gonna do her good," he explained with pride.

Beyond the moments when Hope and I spoke about our dreams, I never really thought about her getting older and having trouble in the world because of her leg. I didn't really know what to think or how to process what he was saying but his tone was so protective and proud, and that stuck with me as I looked back at her through the trees, playing with Lucky.

Ms. Violet was outside hanging clothes on the line when we came walking out of the woods, behind the house. I could see her face light up as she caught us approaching just as Mr. Charlie shouted across the yard.

"I see you, beautiful," he shouted, smiling with love.

"Now jus who you shoutin' at like that?" she shouted back, teasing, as she continued hanging clothes.

"My bride, my bride...ohhh, my, my beautiful bride!" he proclaimed with pride as he raised his hands in the air, firmly gripping the bucket full of fish.

"That bucket better not be empty!" she yelled back without skipping a beat.

I looked up at Mr. Charlie smiling as I walked next to him with a smile on my face; Hope and Lucky were close behind.

"Here you go, Sugar," Mr. Charlie said as he dropped the bucket of fish down on the cutting table.

"Now jus what 'chu suppose she gonna do with all that?" Ms. Violet asked of him.

"Well, she gonna have to clean 'em," he replied, laughing.

"Don't worry none, Sugar, you be as good as any one 'uh them by the time we done," Ms. Violet insisted as she waved her hand at Mr. Charlie, as if to dismiss him.

"Yes ma'am," Hope said in return with a slight smile.

Mr. Charlie set off for work as Hope and Ms. Violet started to clean fish. Ms. Violet was very good at cleaning fish, leaving no bones in the meat while wasting nothing, and she was doing her best to leave Hope with her near flawless technique; and after Hope got over her frustration, she was catching on quite well.

Lucky lingered around the table and kept sampling any falling pieces of fish guts, but would quickly spit them out as he learned how awful it all tasted; although his memory seemed to be quite short and he continued to put his taste to the test each time something new hit the ground.

I tried to help but Ms. Violet wouldn't have it, so I sat down with my back against the tree and watched as Hope got the hand of what she was doing and was quickly putting a dent in the once full bucket of fish. The two of them talked amongst each other like a couple of old women baking bread together, gossiping and swapping knowledge; only it was outside under the early morning sun and it was fish and not flour.

I just listened mostly, not saying very much, as I sat with my eyes closed and a smile on my face.

That evening when I got home from work the backyard was full of people. Ms. Violet and Mr. Charlie were having a fish fry and they must have gotten the word out to the entire congregation because I'd never ever seen that many people in one place outside of our church.

I sifted through bodies as I searched for Hope with Lucky at my side.

"Come, child, eat, eat!" the voice of Ms. Violet spoke out.

I turned around and there was Hope, sitting next to Ms. Violet at the table. As I walked toward them Lucky went off in another direction, most likely to say hello to our visitors and seek out any attention or food he could find.

As I said hello and sat down at the table, Ms. Violet set a plate of food in front of me along with a cold bottle of pop.

"Ma'am?" I asked as I picked up the bottle, staring at it.

"Well, go on now," she insisted with joy, smiling as she flipped her hand at me.

I'd never had pop before. My grandmother would sometimes send me to fetch her tobacco from the general store, and there was always this same small group of older men who seemed to do nothing more than visit and drink pop; I often wondered what it tasted like, but I never found myself so lucky.

"Hope?" I asked, gesturing to offer a taste.

"Sugar and I had our taste, this is for you," Ms. Violet said as she rubbed Hope's back.

I slowly brought the cold, sweating, glass bottle of pop up to my smiling lips. Hope and Ms. Violet were both smiling, equally curious to witness my first taste. I closed my eyes and tilted it back. The cold, sweet, fizzy liquid filled my mouth and tickled its way down my throat; I'd never tasted anything like it.

"How's that?" Ms. Violet asked, smiling with joy as I set the bottle back down on the table.

"Worth all the wonder," I said softly, smiling in return.

"Ain't that right!" she chirped with her unmistakably genuine smile and laugh.

"Sure you don't want some? I don't mind none, I had my taste," I asked of Hope and Ms. Violet.

"No, no, that's awful sweet of you, baby, but you go on, that's yours, you enjoy it," Ms. Violet replied proudly.

"Even if I did, I couldn't...not after seein' the look on your face when you jus had a little taste," Hope said, laughing, as Ms. Violet joined in.

"What's all this for anyway, Ms. Violet?" I asked curiously as I looked around.

"We jus thought it was 'bout time we celebrated a bit more around here, enjoyin' what we got...every bit we been given," she replied, looking at Hope.

"I like that," I stated, smiling, as I took a bite of food.

Soon after, as I was still eating, music began to play. Mr. Charlie played the harmonica and there was a man with a guitar and another with a horn; then another man, who was blind, had a piece of plywood set beneath him on the ground and he began to stomp his feet on it while he slapped his thighs and clapped in beat to the quick but very full sound of music. It was like nothing I'd heard before. I slowly lowered my fork onto my plate and sat still with my eyes closed, listening to each sound as I could feel it crawl under my skin, up and down my entire body. My toes began to tap on the ground beneath them; then my hands, one after the other, joined in slapping against the table, seeking out their rhythm.

"That's right, baby, it's in you, feel it, let it take over your soul," Ms. Violet said as she laughed, clapping her hands.

I opened my eyes; people were dancing all around us. Hope was sitting across from me, smiling, as she watched all of the movement and energy surrounding us. Ms. Violet was clapping her hands in rhythm, smiling, as she swayed from side to side.

I couldn't help myself, I slid out from the table and my feet just started moving across the ground; with my torn shirt, unbuttoned, flowing loosely around me as I twirled in circles, following my feet.

This was music; not like in church where it was guided words. This took over your body, it was knocking on the walls of every inch of my skin and I had to move.

The clapping of a dozen peoples' hands commenced as I opened my eyes to see that everyone had formed a circle around me, smiling and encouraging my movement. As much as I would have liked to stop and duck away with embarrassment, I couldn't stop dancing. I could hear Mr. Charlie shouting *"hey now"* with his smooth tone as he cheered me on in between blowing back and forth across his harmonica with great passion.

Before I knew it, everyone had joined in dancing, with and around me. As my eyes shuttered in slow motion I could see Hope through the crowd, sitting at the table where I'd left her, clapping and smiling from ear to ear as she swayed along to the music with Ms. Violet who was still seated next to her. I waved, and together in perfect timing they waved back proudly, laughing.

Chapter 9

Life was good as time passed by. I was staying busy at work and
Ms. Violet continued to teach me how to save what little earnings I
was making. Hope and I were spending a lot of time together and
she still came out fishing every time we went, even though she
always got stuck with cleaning them. I think she liked the time she
had with Ms. Violet while cleaning fish just as much as she did with
us catching them, so her "losing" was never really a loss. Our little
community fish fry's were becoming a more frequent gathering and
with every one we had the music got right up under my skin and
kept me dancing late into the night. People knew me by name and
as we all ate they would walk by or give a friendly shout across the
yard, asking me if I'd warmed up my legs for the hours ahead. Mr.
Charlie began to teach me how to play the harmonica after he'd
given me one of his old ones; I kept it with me at all times and I
blew on it any chance I had.

Along with the helping hands of Mr. Charlie and the eyes of Hope, I
dug out, framed in, and reinforced a cellar behind the house. We
built a small shed overtop of the entrance to help keep it as cool as
possible; Mr. Nelson gave me everything I needed to do so. He even
let Mr. Charlie and I use one of the flatbed trucks from the yard to
transport the material from the shop to the house. I offered to work
off the cost of everything he'd given me but he insisted that I just
take it. He said that I was a well-mannered, hardworking young
man, and that every now and again a man of such character
deserved *"a break from the system"*, as he put it, slapping me on the
shoulder with reassurance as he winked at me.

My grandmother had taught me how to can, and that's what I did
with most of the vegetables from the garden as they came up,
which I stored in the cellar, and I built a bin along one of the walls
down there for anything I didn't can, particularly the potatoes.

When my grandmother was alive she managed to use up just about everything from the garden, never really having to buy anything. Now, with how I was living, catching fish regularly and buying the odd bit of food from the general store, plus sharing and eating most meals next door, I thought having a cellar full of food was a good idea. Ms. Violet used up any space she desired for her canning and was always welcome to take anything as she pleased. It was all a very good thing.

Mr. Nelson worked a crew on his farm and as he was trying to wrap up the years' crops he was in need of a few extra hands, so I filled my day with work on his farm and then I went to do my regular clean up at the mill in the evening. With the help of Mr. Charlie, we were able to get Hope a job alongside me at the farm during the day. Mr. Nelson was really fond of Mr. Charlie and he seemed to take a liking to me pretty quick, which wasn't the case with everyone, so he paid Hope to make sandwiches for the workers and keep them full of water under the hot fall sun.

Hope's dry sense of humor and work ethic caught the attention of Mr. Nelson after just a few days and he quickly became her biggest fan. It wasn't long before he had her alongside him every chance he could, just to keep him company. When things were falling behind and he gave the boys hell, he would look to Hope as he scolded them, asking her what she thinks should be done. She'd answer with some smart remark and they'd play off of one another with little bits of back and forth as though they had known each other for years. I stayed busy and was often given a separate task or job for the day so I enjoyed their banter, often from a distance, as much as they seemed to.

I knew when they pulled up with Mr. Nelson driving, Lucky in the middle, and Hope on the side, what they were up to. There weren't too many sandwiches or cups filled with water passed around without some sly remarks and teasing of the guys about their work efforts. It was all in good fun though, and as far as I could tell everyone knew that, and most of the guys had a laugh as well as a quick little exchange as they ate through a short but, much needed, break.

Hope seemed to bring a smile to everyone when she came around.

"Hey, Poor Boy, c'mon over here right quick!" Mr. Nelson hollered.

"Yes sir," I shouted as I dropped my pitch fork and went in his direction. "Sir?" I asked as I reached him.

"You got some 'uh that fish you been catchin'…some you can spare?" he asked as he leaned on the back of his truck.

"I can, sir…I can get you some, that ain't no problem. How much you want?" I questioned eagerly, smiling.

"I ain't but one man, son, so, I don't need no more than just one fish," he returned playfully.

"You got it, sir, I can get 'chu that, no sweat!" I replied proudly.

"Just how much you want for one 'uh them fish anyway…you know, just in case I need to dig up some money from under the barn out back," he went on, winking at me.

"For you, sir, free…ain't gonna cost you a cent," I insisted as I shifted to stand in his shadow, working to avoid the sun in my eyes.

"No?!" he questioned with surprise.

"Every good man deserves a break from the system now and again," I stated, smiling.

"Now you catchin' on, son…*atta boy!*" he replied, patting me on the shoulder. "Now why don't you head on home and see if you can't snag me one 'uh them fish?" he added.

"What about work at the yard, sir?" I asked, referring to my evening duties at the mill.

"It ain't goin' nowhere...still be there for you when you can get to it...I'll bet on it," he said as he waved his hand in the air, dismissing my mentioning of it.

"And Hope, sir?" I asked.

"I'll see to it that she ends up where she belongs," he answered, looking over his shoulder at her as she stood talking to one of the men while she filled his cup with water.

"Sounds good, sir...then I'll go get to catchin' you that fish!" I said, eager to get going.

"I'm lookin' forward to it," he replied as he slapped his hand against the side of his truck and walked in the direction of Hope.

I took off running in the opposite direction without giving Hope any indication of my leaving, as I figured I could be back in time with a fish for Mr. Nelson and then be able to walk home with her.

When I got home, Ms. Violet was hanging clothes on the line out back.

"Hey there, sweetheart, where'd you leave Sugar at?" she spoke out with a curious tone.

"She still workin' with Mr. Nelson in the field. He sent me to go catch him a fish and then I'll walk back home with Hope once I get that in his hands," I answered quickly as I was grabbing my rod and bucket.

"She gonna be okay like that...left alone?" she questioned with concern.

"Yes ma'am, don't think she can be bothered by much," I replied with certainty.

"Ain't that jus right," Ms. Violet returned with pride as she smiled.

"Yes ma'am, sure is. I'm gonna get on my way 'n get to catchin' that fish," I said as I took off.

"You be safe, honey!" she shouted.

"Yes ma'am!" I yelled back as I ran into the woods.

I must have cast and come up empty thirty times before I caught my breath from running. The sun was hiding behind some clouds on its slow descent, as evening called, and the fish were being quite picky with their bite. There was a little pool that I knew was a sure thing but I had to balance on a rock that was peeking out of the water in order to get my hook into that particular spot; my only hesitation was that the water was moving quite fast around the rock I was looking to jump onto, and it wasn't very deep, but it was fast. I took a leap and landed with one-foot dead center on the rock while the other was flailing behind me, keeping my balance, as I teetered with my arms out. After about ten seconds of not being sure if I was going to end up in the water, I finally got my balance and was able to swing my hook directly into the pool which I was seeking. The first few casts came up empty and then as soon as the hook hit the water on the next toss I had a bite.

"Got 'em! I knew you was in there!" I shouted in celebration.

I pulled back to snag the catch and just as I yanked up on my rod the fish came flying out of the water, throwing me off balance. As I was falling backward I threw the rod up and over my head and I could see the fish flapping in the air, just as I hit the water.

I remember an instant panic and thinking in that split second that I was going to die. As I bobbed up out of the water I could see how far I'd moved downstream from the rock in just a matter of seconds. I had just enough time to take a deep breath before I went back under. My heart was racing and my mind was scattered, I couldn't think straight. I opened my eyes under the water to try and gain my wits but I couldn't see anything.

"STAND UP!" I heard a voice shout just as I resurfaced.

I started throwing my arms around to try and slow down as I swung my feet under my body in an effort to stand up. I could feel the bottom; my feet were touching the sandy floor beneath me. I managed to hop on the tips of my toes while I used my arms to help steer my body, making my way to the shores edge. I grabbed a hold of the long, deep rooted strands of grass on the bank and I pulled myself up.

As I rolled over and laid on my back, gasping for air, I looked around, searching for the source of the shouting voice. I propped myself up on my elbows to have a better look; nothing, there was no one in sight.

"Hello?" I questioned aloud as I turned my head back and forth.

I sat still for a few minutes, curious to hear an answer or even some movement in the trees but it was quiet; aside from the flowing water, there wasn't anything to be heard.

I stood to my feet and looked around as I made my way back to my bucket and fishing rod. The fish I had flung into midair by the grasp of my hook and line, managed to land right at the waters' edge. It laid struggling for air as its tail slowly flapped up and down on the verge of certain death.

I stood over the fish for a brief moment, staring down at it, and then I kneeled down to pick it up. I pulled the hook out of its mouth and as I crouched at the edge of the water, soaking wet, I held the fish in my hands and then slowly let it slip away, back into the water, as its eyes were filled with new life.

Something just didn't feel right about letting that fish die, or being responsible for its death; not after what I'd just been through.

I picked up my bucket and rod as I stood to my feet and had one last look around for whoever it was that shouted to me. The woods remained silent and still.

I was on my way to get Hope, in a state of great thanks.

I got off the road and cut through the ditch into the field to see if they were still working. There were a few guys left just putting an end to their work, packing everything up and cleaning the equipment for the next day.

"You see where Hope gone off to?" I asked one of the men.

"She gone with Mr. Nelson...'bout a half hour ago," he replied as he stopped to wipe the sweat from his brow.

"Thank you, sir," I said as I continued to walk in the direction of Mr. Nelson's nearby house.

There was a gate left open at the back of Mr. Nelson's property that was being used to enter the yard from the field. I walked through the open space leaving the gate as it was, slowly bouncing on its hinges in the evening breeze, for the men who were finishing up their day.

I heard shouting as I neared the shop where Mr. Nelson's truck was parked. I slowly made my way into the building just as I could hear that it was Hope who was yelling.

"You best jus keep away from me, or you gonna be real sorry, I swear by it!" she shouted as I saw the frame of a man with his back to me.

"Jus go on and put that down you little cripple, you gonna hurt yourself," the man taunted her, laughing, as she swung a pitch fork from side to side in an effort to keep him at a distance.

My entire body flooded with anger as I could feel the vulnerability in Hope's voice. And even though she was putting up a fearless front as she swung that pitch fork back and forth, it angered me to the bone to see her being backed into a corner with no way out.

I quietly stepped back outside and grabbed a shovel that was leaning against the wall by the shop door. I walked back in, holding it with two hands up above my head, and I swung it with everything I had.

"Poor Boy!" Hope shouted, while the sharp '*ping*' dented the air just as the man turned his head to see me.

Everything happened so fast and by the time he'd turned his head from Hope yelling my name, I was in full motion with my swing. I watched his eyes roll into the back of his head as it twisted from the impact of the shovel and he fell onto his side.

I dropped the shovel, grabbed Hope by the hand and helped guide her around the mans' body as he laid still on the floor.

I didn't let go of her hand until we were half way to home, neither of us speaking a word the entire time.

We stopped to rest for a few minutes next to a tree in the tall grass alongside the road.

"You alright?" I asked as she was favoring her leg, leaning against the tree.

"Yeah...I'm fine," she insisted, cringing, appearing to be in pain. "You okay?" she asked.

"I'm okay," I replied, nodding my head as I caught my breath.

She smiled ever so slightly.

"Ain't that a sight," I suggested, pointing into the distance as I chuckled.

"Where you suppose he comin' from?" Hope asked as she laughed.

Lucky was running toward us with the sun lowering behind him as he barked repeatedly to gain our attention.

Hope and I laughed in harmony as the sight and sound of our young friend brought a much needed warmth to the air. Lucky barreled over Hope as he reached us, making her fall into the tall grass. It was as though he knew what had happened and was just so happy to see her unharmed.

The two of them played in one another's affection as I smiled and laughed, eventually dropping to my knees to join in.

When I got into the house, after Hope and I parted ways for the night, I warmed some water for a bath. Just before I undressed I went into my grandmothers' room, grabbed her perfume, and I left trails of it throughout the house. The scent was comforting as I scrubbed my skin while Lucky sat on the floor next to me, getting splashed with warm soapy water.

It wasn't very often that I needed any sort of comforting, but there was something about having a warm bath after a long and dirty day and the smell of my grandmothers' perfume wafting throughout the house that brought an ease over me.

CHAPTER 10

The next morning, I woke to a heavy handed knock at the back door.

"Morning, sir," I said, squinting, as I opened the door to see it was Mr. Nelson.

Before he even replied he had me on my heels walking backwards as he barged into the house without hesitation. My heart began to race; I was sure he sought me out to get to the bottom of what happened the day before.

"You got somethin' you might wanna tell me, son?" he questioned, looking around as he took his hat off and sat it down on the kitchen table.

"Sir?" I replied in question.

"You sure now?" he asked as he sat down.

"Can I fix you some coffee...or tea?" I asked as I opened the back door to let Lucky out after he greeted Mr. Nelson.

"There ain't no need to be lying to me, son, we've got an understanding, you and I...do we not?" he stated as he hammered his index finger against the surface of the kitchen table.

I stood still, wearing nothing but my underwear, with my hands tucked into the waistband as I stared at him, uncertain of what to say.

"This about not gettin' you that fish?" I asked. "'Cause I was gonna...I was, I was there, I jus fell in the water is all and I los' the one I had for you, but I can go get you another one," I stammered nervously.

"How you suppose you gonna do that when your rod and bucket is sittin' in the back of my truck?" he asked as he pointed outside.

"Sir?" I questioned.

"It was on the ground, just outside the shop, right where you left it. Now look, son, I didn't come here lookin' for no mish mash 'uh stories from you, I feel like I always been fair to you, straight from the get go...and now I expect the same in return. I coulda' gone another route to get to the bottom of all this but I didn't...so why don't you just take yourself a deep breath and tell me what happened," he spoke sternly.

"I hit 'im...I hit 'im with a shovel that I found leaning against the building," I blurted out, looking down at the floor.

"Now what on earth are you gonna tell me would possess a young man like yourself to go and hit someone across the head with a steel shovel? How you gonna make sense 'uh this for me?" he asked as he pulled the chair out beside him and patted his hand on it, gesturing for me to sit down.

"He alright?" I questioned as I slowly sat down on the chair.

*"No he ain't alright, he ain't nowhere **near** bein' alright...he halfway to bein' a cripple,"* he stated firmly.

"Huh?" I asked, looking up at him.

"You musta' rattled his brain loose, son, he ain't got a single word to mutter. Only reason I know to come here is 'cause the boys saw you scatter; said you and little Miss Hope was clearin' outta there like you just set the place on fire," he explained as he waved his hand back and forth.

All I could think about is when I heard that man taunting Hope, calling her a cripple.

"That sure wasn't my meaning when I grabbed a hold 'uh that shovel, sir, but I can't say he didn't have it comin' to him," I said with certainty as I looked him in the eyes.

For every whooping I caught from my grandmother over the years I never witnessed an ounce of sorrow in her eyes for doing so. She made the decision, she followed through, and she stuck by it.

"You wanna explain that to me?" he asked, reaching over and grabbing a hold of my upper arm.

"Mr. Nelson...." I said, cringing, as he began to squeeze my arm.

He continued to hold his grip on my arm as he stared into my eyes. He was trying to pressure me into speaking but I had already made up my mind that I wasn't going to say anything more about it. I didn't want to get Hope involved and I knew by how he was looking at me that it really didn't matter what I said next, and nothing would change what happened.

"You know I can't have you workin' for me no more, I don't tolerate that kinda behavior from the men and I certainly won't do it from a child. Thought you was better than all this, thought I saw a lot 'uh good in you, and I can't say that I ain't disappointed about it all," he explained as he slowly let go of my arm.

"I understand," I replied, standing to my feet.

"Any reason I should be talkin' to little Hope about all this?" he asked as he stood up, grabbing his hat off the table.

"No sir, she ain't got nothin' to do with it...was all my doin'," I answered, shaking my head slowly.

"Well then...." he started as he opened the back door to head outside.

"Sir...." I interrupted.

He stopped walking, turning back to me.

"Thank you for bein' so kind to me…and for all that you done when you never had to," I said, squinting with one eye as I tilted my head.

He nodded and smiled. Not saying another word, he grabbed my rod and bucket from the back of his truck, walked it over to lean it on the back step and then he got into his truck and drove away.

Lucky came running back in the house just as I was about to close the door. I tucked the chairs back in under the kitchen table and went to lie down on the couch.

As I laid there thinking about what I was going to do with my days now that I didn't have a job, my mind wandered off and I fell asleep.

"Hey, hey, Poor Boy…you up?" I woke to the whisper of Hope's voice.

As I laid on my side, I opened one eye to see her hunched over me.

"Up, yeah, I'm up…" I replied with my mouth buried in the cushion of the couch.

"You late for work. That a choice you make over what happened, or you jus oversleep?" she asked.

"Nah, I ain't gonna work there no more," I replied, pushing myself up off the couch.

"You ain't?" she asked.

She walked over and sat down in my grandmothers' chair. My vision blurred for a brief moment as I looked at her, blending into the chair that was only ever visited by the body of my grandmother. I shook my head back and forth rapidly, adjusting my perception of reality.

"You okay?" Hope questioned, sounding concerned.

"I'm fine, yeah, I'm, I'm okay," I stammered.

"Well if you ain't goin' back to work then I sure ain't goin' back there," she stated.

"What 'chu gonna say to Mr. Charlie about this," I asked, sitting across the room at the kitchen table.

"Jus gonna tell the truth...that place ain't for me," she replied, shrugging her shoulders. "You?" she asked.

"I'm jus gonna wait 'till he come home and see what he got to say," I said as I stood up, scratching my belly.

"Yeaah...good thinkin'," she replied, nodding her head as she pointed her index finger at me.

"And Ms. Violet...you say anything to her?" I asked.

"Nah, I didn't have to, she jus happy to see me stick around in the morning. She worry too much about me anyway, so she ain't gonna mind none if I don't work," Hope explained, still seated in my grandmothers' chair.

"Yeah...she sure does love you. I ain't never seen a woman look at nobody the way she look at you," I suggested as I walked over to the couch and began folding my blankets.

"Gimme that," Hope demanded as she stood up, bent over and grabbed a hold of one end of my blanket to help me fold it.

We flipped it around a few times to match the seams, as Hope was instructing me, folded it in the air as we had it stretched out, and then Hope walked toward me with her end. That was the first time I'd ever had any help folding my blankets.

"Who taught you that?" I asked, smiling, as I laid the blanket at the foot of the couch.

"Don't know, jus made sense I guess...after watchin' you fumble around with it," she answered, straight faced.

I shook my head and laughed as the two of us walked across the room into the kitchen. Hope sat down at the table as I put some water on to boil for tea. Lucky followed her every move within the house and finally made his way to her side, on the floor, by the kitchen table.

I grabbed the back of a chair from the table and I slid it across the floor. I climbed up onto the counter and I pulled out a jar filled with sugar cubes that my grandmother had stashed in the back of a cupboard.

My grandmother would use one each evening in her tea while she had a cigarette before she went to bed. She never let me have a taste so I completely forgot about them until the water started to boil.

Hope's eyes lit up like two moons as soon as I turned around and set the jar down on the countertop.

"You like sugar in your tea?" I asked, laughing, as I carried the jar over to the table.

Hope started to laugh.

"How many you put in?" she asked, still laughing.

"Many as you want," I replied, smiling, as I opened the jar.

I filled two cups with boiling water and I carried them over to the table.

Hope had her eyes locked on to the jar of sugar cubes as I placed a teabag in each cup, along with a spoon.

"Should we maybe have jus 'uh piece while the water cools?" I asked as I could see the temptation in her eyes.

"I mean, couldn't hurt...right?" Hope replied, shrugging her shoulders.

I grabbed the jar and tilted it toward her, gesturing for her to stick her hand in and grab some; which she did. Slowly, she reached in, flipping her eyes back and forth between me and the sugar, and she pinched a single piece between her thumb and index finger then pulled it out.

"Go on...taste it," I said, smiling, as I set the jar upright.

"Ain't you havin' none?" she asked.

"I will...*you first*," I replied, staring at her in anticipation of her reaction.

She guided her hand to her mouth and gently placed the cube of sugar onto her tongue. Slowly closing her eyes, she touched her lips together and smiled.

I stood, leaning on the table, propped up on my elbows, staring at her as her smile continued to stretch across her pretty face with each passing second.

A single tear fell from her left eye as her lips quivered.

"What is it...what's wrong?" I asked hesitantly, not wanting to upset her.

"Don't know...was jus havin' some memories...thinkin' 'bout my momma; felt like I was right there next to her," she explained, slowly opening her eyes.

"You ever think about finding her?" I asked softly.

"Nah...she don't wanna see me. Why you think I'm here?" she replied, wiping the single tear from her cheek.

I grabbed the jar of sugar and slid it back and forth between my hands on the table in front of her, enticing her to take another; and so she did.

I sat down at the table and we each had some sugar. Hope didn't say another word about her mother and I didn't ask.

We didn't talk too much, but that was mostly because our mouth's stayed pretty full. Each taking a turn, one after another, sliding a hand into the jar and scooping out another piece of sugar to slowly set upon our tongues.

Before we knew it, the jar was empty.

Neither of us could sit still so as we found ourselves laughing uncontrollably at Lucky while he laid still on the kitchen floor looking up at us, appearing to be confused, we decided to go outside for a walk to the creek.

Walking through the forest we continued to laugh with very little cause.

We sat down against a big, old tree and we took turns prodding and berating Lucky with questions about his attitude and home life; making light of our own uncertainties and displeasures within each of our lives. Knowing full well he couldn't respond to it seemed to give a certain playful release to life. Hope would raise her voice as she spoke out toward her mother, as did I, while Lucky stared at each of us in brief moments balanced with what appeared to be a slight understanding and then also complete confusion.

As our energy from the sugar was fading, the blurting out of words started to carry a different tone and emotion.

"Why didn't you want me?" Hope shouted at Lucky as a tear fell from her eye.

She stood to her feet.

"What'd I do wrong, huh?" she continued. *"Was it that hard 'tuh love me?"* she yelled as she looked to the sky with her arms out to her side.

Lucky looked over at me as I stood to my feet.

Hope began to gasp for breath as she continued to belt out her frustrations and feelings of despair into the treetops above.

"You okay?" I asked, just as she took a deep breath, turning to look at me.

"Huh?" she replied as her eyes rolled into the back of her head and she collapsed, falling to the ground.

"Hope!" I belted out as I tried to catch her before she hit the ground.

Lucky started to whimper as I dropped to my knees at her side while I continued to shout her name.

She laid motionless with her eyes closed as I began to panic, shaking her from side to side as gently as I could manage.

"Hope...Hope, wake up! Hope, you in there...c'mon, get up now, we gotta get home, Ms. Violet's gonna be worried," I spoke out, raising my voice as I kneeled, watching her anxiously.

I looked up toward the path where we had entered the forest, and then looked back down at Hope. As moments passed and she continued in the same state my concern grew, as did my uncertainty for what needed to be done. I didn't want to leave her side in case she woke up but with each passing second I was sure that something needed to happen.

I grabbed her by the arm and slowly tried to stand up. Her body was completely limp which was making it difficult to keep my balance. I lowered her back down to the ground. I tried again with no success, as I grunted, letting out a loud sigh of frustration.

Lucky started to bark.

"I can't, I can't...she ain't gonna let me," I said to Lucky as he continued to bark at me.

I looked up to the blue sky as the sun was shining down in a break through the treetops.

I filled my lungs with a long, deep breath and with one swift motion I swung her arm up and over my shoulder. As I managed to keep my balance, not skipping a beat, I began walking with her in my arms. Lucky was quick to follow.

It wasn't long before I was covered in sweat and was quickly losing my grip. As I struggled to keep her in my grasp, I continued home, shifting my upper body backward in order to shuffle her tight against my chest.

I made my way out of the woods and picked up the pace as I was clear to move through the grass without any obstacles. My left hand was burning with pain and I could feel the moisture running down my arm, dripping from my elbow. Soon, my whole left side from the waist down was wet, which was causing me to lose my grip, but then I laid eyes on Ms. Violet at the back of the house, tending to whatever task was at hand.

"Ms. Violet...." I muttered as loud as I could in a short breath.

"Child...what've you two done now?" she belted out as she came to meet me.

"I ain't done nothin', she jus took a spell 'n won't get up," I replied as I neared her open arms.

"C'mon now, let's get her in the house," she said as she grabbed a hold of Hope's legs to help carry her inside.

We got her in through the back door, into the living room, and we laid her down on the couch.

Ms. Violet was quick to scramble around getting a wash pan filled with water while she had me put the kettle on to boil.

"Baby, what've you done to yourself?" she asked of me, concerned.

"Ma'am?" I replied in question.

"You full 'uh blood, sweetheart," she said, pointing to my leg.

Just as I looked down at my leg, my left arm felt like it caught a cool breeze. Blood was dripping down my arm, into my hand, and onto the floor. My left leg was stained in blood, as was my shoe. I looked at my arm and could see deep into the flesh as it appeared to have rubbed off.

Carrying Hope the way that I was had her leg brace against my arm, and the movement of steps and gripping her tightly must have worn at my skin. I thought as I was panicking and struggling to hold her that it was sweat dripping down my side but now seeing it, that clearly wasn't the case.

"I guess it happen when I was bringin' her home," I suggested, looking at my arm and then up at Ms. Violet.

"Honey, you bes' be gettin' a towel on that so we can tend ta' Sugar," she insisted with care.

"Yes ma'am," I replied as I scurried around the kitchen, cupping my arm with my opposite hand.

I grabbed a towel off the counter and dampened it with cold water, at the instruction of Ms. Violet, then wrapped it around my arm while she continued to softly summon Hope with words of love.

"C'mon, Sugar...you come on back to us, you hear me," she spoke with conviction as she laid a cool, damp cloth upon the forehead of Hope.

She didn't wake.

Mr. Charlie soon arrived at home, and with great concern he never took his eyes off of Hope. As he stayed at Hope's side, Ms. Violet sat me down at the kitchen table and had a closer look at my arm.

"You a real special child, sweetheart," she said kindly as she gently shook her head, looking at my arm.

"Ma'am?" I questioned.

"You done a number on your arm, baby, and you gonna need some thread to pull this back to form," she explained, cupping my face with her hands.

"Yes ma'am," I replied simply.

While Ms. Violet gathered everything she needed and filled a basin with warm water, I went into the next room to check on Hope.

"She gonna be okay, right?" I questioned Mr. Charlie.

"Can only wait...but she gotta' big, stubborn heart, jus like her grandmother...so ain't no spell gonna keep her under for long," he replied as he winked, sitting at Hope's side with her hand wrapped tightly in his grip.

He never asked me what happened or showed any interest in the circumstances of Hope ending up in the state that she was, nor did I look for the space to explain.

"Ms. Violet gonna fix that up?" he asked, looking to my arm.

"Yes sir, she jus getting together what she need," I replied, nodding as I stood still, staring at Hope.

"She gonna be fine," he spoke up, in tune with my concern.

"Yeah, she gonna be jus fine," I said slowly, smiling.

"C'mon, sit, sweetheart, sit down...let's get 'chu fixed up," Ms. Violet called from the kitchen.

"Yes ma'am," I replied as I turned to go see her.

As I approached the kitchen table where she sat waiting, slowly spinning the tip of a needle between her fingers over the flame of a thick white candle, I took a deep breath and sat down next to her.

"Go on 'n soak your arm in there," she instructed me as she pointed to the washbasin on the table.

It immediately began to burn. As I sat up in my chair, Ms. Violet put one hand on my lap and spoke soft, loving words to calm me.

After my arm soaked for a few minutes in her saltwater concoction, she poured some clean, warm water over the wound and then gently patted it dry.

"Now, I ain't gonna suga'coat nothin', baby, this is gonna sting some," Ms. Violet explained in a calm tone as she rolled the tip of the threaded needle over the flame.

"Yes ma'am, I understand," I replied as I looked away.

"You want one 'uh Mr. Charlie's old straps to put in there between your teeth?" she asked, smiling. "I'd give you a swill 'uh brandy if we had any, but..." she added with a wink.

"I'll be okay," I answered, smiling in return.

She gave me one last warning of the impending pain and the advice to keep my eyes distracted, and then all I remember is wishing I had taken something to bite down on.

I'd never experienced a pain so sharp, quite so fast. I'm not sure if it was the heat of the needle or the cinching of my skin as she tugged it tight with each cross, but I'm certain I had an array of facial expressions never before seen.

She talked me through each moment while I did my best to not look, as I could already picture every millimeter of thread being strung through my arm as though I was watching.

Once Ms. Violet was finished the stitching, she hunched down over my arm, gripped one end of the thread between her teeth and pulled tight with her free hand while she held her finger over the cinched wound; she bit the thread and then spit into the washbasin where my arm once soaked.

"All done, sweetheart. You sure quite a young man about life, child, you jus take it all as it comes...you somethin' else, baby, you sure are," Ms. Violet spoke as she gently rinsed my arm one last time.

"Thank you, ma'am, thank you for fixin' me up, and thank you for always bein' so kind to me," I replied, smiling.

She smiled, patted her hands dry on the apron she wore over her dress, cupped my face, and kissed me on the forehead.

After she wrapped a bandage around my arm she sent me into the next room to check on Hope and Mr. Charlie while she tidied up in the kitchen.

Hope hadn't yet woken, and Mr. Charlie was still yet to leave her side.

Ms. Violet soon joined us with some tea and the three of us sat visiting deep into the night, listening to Mr. Charlie's stories, huddled around Hope as she laid still.

Chapter 11

I woke up the next morning on the floor next to the sofa where Hope laid; the house was quiet. I sat up to have a look at Hope, only to find her in the same state as the night before. I whispered her name a few times and gently shook her arm but she didn't budge; I began to worry. I held my left hand an inch or so over her mouth and nose, just to ease my mind. Clearly she was still breathing, as her warm breath was beating against my chilled hand; although it didn't seem to calm my mind. I gently shook her again, and then again. As my whispers turned to quick belts of noise, she remained unbothered.

"Why don't you jus go on 'n drag her across the floor?" the voice of Mr. Charlie chimed in from behind me as he entered the room.

"Sir?" I asked, turning my head to see him.

"Well if she ain't gonna wake like that, maybe she need a little bump," he added, smiling, seemingly at ease.

"I uhhh...." I started.

"Oh would you leave that poor child alone," Ms. Violet spoke up as she came out from the back room.

"Good mornin', ma'am," I said, snickering, happy to see her.

"Mornin', darlin'. How you feelin', how's your arm?" she asked as she leaned over, gently resting her hand on the forehead of Hope.

"I'm good, it's uh, it's good," I replied, watching keenly, waiting for Hope to respond.

"She sure tired," Ms. Violet said, looking at Mr. Charlie.

"Would seem so," he replied as he rolled up the sleeves on his shirt.

I sat waiting, listening to the two of them talk back and forth about the day to come while Ms. Violet began to prepare breakfast.

The three of us sat down to eat, although I didn't have much of an appetite. Instead, I played with my food while I continued to keep my eyes locked on Hope, as she was in plain view from where I sat, restless, at the table.

They could sense my anxiety and it wasn't long before Ms. Violet rested her hand on mine, while she and Mr. Charlie both assured me that Hope would be okay and that if her current state didn't change in due time, they would seek out medical attention.

I myself had never been to a doctor or even knew of one, I was just happy to hear their concern be vocalized.

Mr. Charlie got his things together, kissed Hope on the cheek, wished her well, and was off to work after parting with Ms. Violet, leaving her with a kiss as well. With Hope being in such condition it didn't seem right that we talk about work or what transpired in my being relieved of my duties at the farm, so he said a simple goodbye after teasing me about my arm, and he was on his way.

Over the course of the day, I waited within an eyes' view for Hope to wake. Ms. Violet tended to her daily tasks of baking and cleaning house, keeping busy, both inside and out. She didn't seem too concerned about the state of Hope, or maybe that was just my perception, as I was anticipating anything, even something as small as her moving around in her sleep.

As suppertime neared, Ms. Violet sent me home to check on Lucky, and I did as she asked, but I gave her very clear instructions to shout for me if Hope was to wake while I was gone.

Lucky wasn't anywhere to be found when I crossed the yard getting home, so I set out calling for him as I cupped my hands around my mouth.

"Luuuccckkkyyy, c'mon boy, where you at?" I repeated as I headed toward the bush.

Continuing to call out for him, I kept peering back over my shoulder to see if Ms. Violet was in sight, calling for my return to the house.

I slowly made my way into the woods and as the sun was making its way down for the day, it was becoming difficult to see in the trees.

"You lost, boy?" a voice questioned.

"Who's there?!" I shouted, startled.

"You lose something?" the voice asked.

"Come out here, lemme have a look at 'chu," I demanded.

"Can't nothing be too lucky if you shouting at it like that; you upsetting the whole forest with that racket," he said as he appeared from behind a tree.

"I ain't got nothin' 'tuh hide," I said as I stood as tall as I could.

"No, don't suppose you would by the looks 'uh you," he suggested with ease.

"I know you, mister?" I asked of him, tilting my head to one side.

"You don't remember me?" he asked, taking a step closer into the last bit of light from the setting sun.

"Mister Prophet, that you?" I returned in question.

"It's is," he replied softly, nodding. "What'd you do to your arm?" he asked.

"This...it ain't nothin'," I replied, looking down at my arm. "Why you lurkin' 'round the woods, sir?" I asked, squinting to have a better look at him.

"It ain't so much lurkin' when no one else around," he answered as he fiddled with something in his hands.

"You see my dog through here...you see him, you see Lucky?" I questioned curiously.

"I ain't seen nobody but you," he replied, looking around.

"Luuuccckkkyyy!" I shouted once more.

"Easy with that!" he demanded, stepping back.

"But I need him...and I gotta get home," I explained, looking up at him.

"Why the hurry?" he asked.

"My friend, Hope...she took a spell 'n she ain't come to yet, she still out," I replied as I let out a sigh, concerned.

"And what, you wanna be there when she does, when she comes around?" he asked, leaning back against a tree as he slid a sliver of wood into his mouth.

"'Uh 'course," I replied quickly.

"What if she don't, what if she don't come to?" he suggested calmly.

"Mister...why would you say somethin' like that?" I asked, irritated by his approach. *"Thought you had more sense 'n kindness in you than to say somethin' so thickheaded,"* I finished, feeling unsettled.

"This is about the truth, this ain't about no kindness," he stated, pushing himself off the tree.

"What 'chu mean...the truth?" I questioned curiously.

"You ever lose someone before?" he asked as he stood just a few feet away from me.

"Yes sir," I replied plainly.

"It hurts...don't it?" he prodded.

"It can, sir, at times," I answered.

"Well this ain't about that girl, and it ain't about who you lost or who you may or may not lose...this is about you," he spoke with conviction.

"Ain't sure I follow," I said, confused.

"What exactly you getting from that girl that got you so scared to lose?" he inquired.

"Don't know...we jus friends is all; we laugh 'n mess around, and I guess, well, I guess maybe she jus makes time a bit easier," I replied in truth but uncertain of my answer.

"Makes time easier...what, you got it rough, you got a tough life?" he questioned sternly.

"No sir, no rougher than most folks," I answered without hesitation.

"Listen, life is gonna do what it's set out to do, but...when you can't be bothered inside, when you good no matter what the world gives you or rips away from you...you gonna be exactly who you suppose to be, and there ain't no two ways about it," he insisted as he knelt down and grabbed a handful of soil.

I saw that he was still in bare feet, just as he was the first time we'd met. If it wasn't for the spot in which he chose to kneel I wouldn't have noticed, but the fading sun had found him, as it too was kneeling down, in harmony with time.

Urgency slowed to a point of little interest as I listened to him speak. Although his tone and approach were both slightly brash, his words traveled beyond a thought, much like with the love that Ms. Violet possessed when she spoke.

"Thing is, Hope...she the only friend I got. Well, besides Lucky, but it would seem like he gone now too," I said as I scanned the forest, throwing my arms up in the air. "Ms. Violet and Mr. Charlie, you know, they jus so kind to me, been so ever since I was little but they, well they jus ain't like Hope...they love me, I know they do, but Hope's my friend...only real one I ever had," I explained with care.

"You just gotta keep good in your heart, keep fillin' it with every little bit 'uh hope you can muster up, waste no worry on things you can't control, and you gonna be alright...bright as the moon," he said as he stood up, filling his pocket with the soil from his hand, nodding at me and then turning to walk away.

"Mister Prophet, sir?" I let out.

"Go on," he replied, turning back to look at me.

"I gonna see you again sometime?" I asked, working to keep my eyes on him.

"Don't trouble yourself with such things, son...ain't nobody gonna be able to answer that, not but God his'self, and even he ain't gonna let you in on his secrets," he replied as he turned, walking away.

"G'night, mister Prophet, sir. And sir...if you run in'ta that pup 'uh mine, you do me a favor and send him on home, he gonna be lonely out here on his own, *I can bet,*" I spoke loudly as I stood up on the tips of my toes.

He didn't reply, and as far as I could see he didn't so much as turn to acknowledge what I said. I shrugged my shoulders, kicked a branch that was lying at my feet and then turned around and began heading back to the house.

As I was cutting back through the tall grass, in view of the house, Lucky came barreling at me from across the field, barking. Off in the distance I could see a faint silhouette on the horizon of what appeared to be Prophet coming out of the woods, crossing the field; I waved but he didn't see me.

Lucky was quick to reach me, tackling me as I fell to my backside in the grass while he ended up on my stomach, licking my face with a greeting like I'd never received. We rolled around in the grass and dirt until the sun had finished its duty for the day and then we slowly got up and made our way, side by side, back home.

Ms. Violet was outside, singing into the crisp evening air.

"Where'd you get off to, sweetheart, you was gone for some time?" she asked, breaking to pause from her tune.

"Was out on the hunt for him, ma'am," I replied, pointing back at Lucky as he was sitting, gnawing on his back paw.

"What's he got 'round his neck?" she questioned, flicking her wrist, pointing.

"Don't know, ma'am, jus seen it when I found him...or when he found me," I answered, scratching my back as I turned to look at him.

"Ain't that somethin'," she stated.

I knelt down in front of Lucky, grabbing onto the string below his jaw where it was tied around his neck, seeing that there was something hanging from it. I slid it up and around to his back to have a better look as Ms. Violet walked over to share in the moment.

"Look at that, where'd you suppose he get this?" she asked curiously.

"Not too sure, ma'am...what's it read?" I returned, sharing in her curiosity.

"Have a try," she suggested, nudging my shoulder.

"Can't make it out," I quickly replied.

"Says *'home'*...far as I can see," she said, bewildered.

It was a little round piece of bronze that was quite weather beaten. The edge was rough and it looked like someone had worked to scratch the word 'home' across the face of it and then punched a nail through it to thread the string in one side and out the other.

"Funny thing to see...wonder who gone 'n done that for him," she expressed, curiously.

"Can't think 'uh no one, or where he'd even end up to get such a thing," I added.

"Funny thing," she said, turning away to continue her singing.

"Who'd you run into, boy?" I whispered to Lucky as I slowly stood up.

I took Lucky back home, across the yard, and returned for supper at Ms. Violet's request.

When I got back, Mr. Charlie was sitting on his bench, smoking his pipe, appearing to be in waiting.

"So?" he questioned, puffing on his pipe.

"Sir?" I replied, scratching my shoulder as I neared.

"You know anything about this?" he asked, nodding his head to one side, gesturing toward the house.

"'Bout what, sir?" I asked, turning back as I heard Lucky bark.

"This waiting thing she want us to do," he said.

"No sir, she jus told me to come back for dinner," I replied, unsure of his lead.

Ms. Violet came outside holding a small tub filled with steaming water. She kicked the door closed behind her with the heel of her foot, spilling some of the water on the ground.

"What's this all about?" Mr. Charlie asked, knocking his pipe empty against the sole of his boot.

I moved to help Ms. Violet set the tub of water down on the table.

"Thank you, baby," she said, smiling at me.

"You're welcome," I said in return as she positioned herself to speak.

"That young girl in there, our precious little Hope...she's tired, she ain't well, *and I'll be damned if anyone steps foot in this home with anything but the clear intention on her getting better; and that ain't gonna be through no worry, and it ain't gonna be through a poor train 'uh thought, or even a days' events brought home on your clothes...now strip down and wash up!*" she demanded, handing myself and Mr. Charlie each a cloth then nodding toward the tub.

I never heard her curse before and I had to stop myself from giggling as she said it. I probably could have gotten away with it had the circumstance been different, but in this case she was quite stern with her demand and I didn't want to catch a smack across the back of my head.

Mr. Charlie and I, simultaneously, began to strip down and wash ourselves. He winked at me as he pulled his smile back across his face in an effort to acknowledge Ms. Violet's message.

She stood, watching as we scrubbed our bare bodies from head to toe in the cool evening air.

Handing us each a towel, she smiled, then instructed us to dump out the water and come into the house for supper; she went in ahead of us.

"What 'chu think about that?" Mr. Charlie asked as we tipped over the tub of water.

"Don't know," I replied simply.

"I think it's best if we jus do as she say," he suggested, smiling.

"I think you right," I agreed, smiling in return.

The three of us sat at the kitchen table eating supper while Hope was in the next room on the sofa, just as I'd last seen her.

Ms. Violet was very insistent on us sharing stories of our day and speaking only with positive words. *"Energy is very important in these times,"* she explained.

It was slightly awkward at first as Mr. Charlie and I were still without any clothes on, while Ms. Violet sat fully clothed in her days' attire, but I soon forgot about it and was caught up in the laughter and each passing moment. I didn't speak at all about Prophet and our time in the woods, although I was feeling anxious to share it with someone.

Once supper was finished Ms. Violet sent me home to put on some clean clothes, just as she had sent Mr. Charlie into the back room to do the same.

I came back in a clean pair of underwear with nothing else on, as I had no clean clothes.

I sat down on the floor next to the sofa where Hope was while Ms. Violet and Mr. Charlie were in the kitchen, tidying up.

As I stared at Hope, just inches from her face, I began to whisper, telling her about my meeting Prophet in the woods; I stopped myself as I was talking about how brash he was and I went back to my first introduction with him, as though it would help make more sense for her. It felt good to finally tell someone but, it had just dawned on me that I never questioned him about my fall in the shop.

Once they were finished cleaning up in the kitchen Mr. Charlie came and sat down across from Hope, just to simply watch her. I stood up and went into the kitchen to visit with Ms. Violet.

"You alright, sweetheart?" she asked of me.

"Yes ma'am, I'm okay," I replied as I sat at the table, watching her.

"You jus keep yourself an eye out for miracles, baby, you'll find 'em in the darnedest of places...and they have their way," she insisted, turning back to look at me as her hands were mixing something together in a bowl.

I smiled at her and then looked back at Hope, lying still. I didn't have much experience with miracles, as it was, but I took note of Ms. Violet's words and was sure that I wouldn't miss one if it came my way.

After watching Ms. Violet work in the kitchen for a short time, I went into the next room and sat beside Hope. Mr. Charlie excused himself and went outside.

I woke up the next morning under a blanket, on the floor, at the side of the sofa; the house was quiet. I sat up and looked over at Hope; she still hadn't moved in the slightest.

I stood to my feet, folded the blanket and stacked it with the pillow and then quietly made my way home with my clothes in hand, after picking them up from the back porch.

The sun wasn't up quite yet as I walked across the wet grass from a dew that had set through the night. Lucky greeted me as I neared the house.

I got myself dressed and then grabbed an old, small suitcase from the floor of my grandmothers' closet. Carrying the suitcase, I went outside to the cellar and tossed in some food then went back into the house to gather a few other items. Into the suitcase I added the harmonica that Mr. Charlie had given me, a jacket which belonged to my grandfather, along with one of his hats, a bottle of my grandmothers' perfume, and a small piece of mirror from my grandmothers' dresser drawer.

Lucky sat waiting for me by the back door as he seemed to know we were getting ready to go somewhere. I wrote a small note reading, "bee bak sune", incase Ms. Violet worried; I left it on the kitchen table, closed the door behind me and grabbed my fishing rod, then set out with Lucky at my side.

I didn't know where I was headed but I knew that I needed to go in order for Hope to have any chance.

CHAPTER 12

After cutting across fields and through the bush to keep out of sight from anyone I might know, I came to a road at the edge of town and stuck to the shoulder as I continued to walk along.

Lucky would wander off course, leaving my side for brief periods of time, and each time he returned he greeted me as though he'd been gone for days. I enjoyed his company and cheerful demeanor, but after a few times of him acting like we'd just met after a long absence from one another, it began to wear on me. It wasn't long before I lost my nerve and asked him what his problem was but, him being a dog, he had no response.

We slowly made our way out of view from town; it was the first time I'd ever traveled so far.

As the sun made its way into the sky, Lucky and I stopped at a crossroad to have a snack. A car was nearing from a distance with a trail of dust quick to keep up at its behind. Fearful of not being noticed, I stood up and stepped back, grabbing my suitcase in one hand and a tuff of fur on Lucky's back with the other to keep him calm and out of the way.

The car didn't appear to be slowing down so I took a few more steps back and continued to watch as it approached. As quick as it reached me it passed me, and as it did the driver held the horn down, honking steadily as it sped by. In a split second as it passed me, the driver and I locked eyes, with him winking and smiling at me from the corner of his mouth, waving one hand, as he held down the horn with the other. For as fast as he was traveling, time still managed to slow to a point of allowing such a moment. He didn't look at all familiar but he appeared to be quite young.

As I stood still on the side of the road, not moving an inch, I was soon blinded by a cloud of thick dust. I held tightly onto Lucky, squinting in an effort to see as I could suddenly hear the sound of sirens quickly approaching. Just as the dust was beginning to settle I saw a police car coming in my direction at a fast pace. Again, as quick as the car made its way to where I stood, suitcase in one hand, gripping Lucky with the other, it was gone. With its sirens blaring as loud as could be, it left me in yet another thick cloud of dust.

"Wonder what all the fuss about," I spoke out, still with my vision clouded, covered in dust.

With the dust beginning to clear, I let loose of Lucky and we began our travels once again.

We came upon a store at the roadside just a few miles beyond where we had stopped to eat. There were men gathered out front, seated along the front wall, while one stood on his feet holding the attention of the entire group. There were small breaks of laughter as we neared while the men anticipated the next pairing of words to come.

"What 'chu suppose they laughin' at?" I asked of Lucky, looking down at him as he appeared just as interested.

"Hey, boy, come here, come settle this for us," one man shouted. *"Would you?"* he added.

"Sir?" I replied, rubbing my eyes as they were still quite dry.

"He ain't gonna be able to say, he got no idea, he jus a kid," another man spoke up.

"Nah, take a look at him...he on his way somewhere, he's well traveled...ain't 'cha boy?" the man who was standing up spoke loudly.

"I can try my best, sir," I said in return as I slowly joined the group.

"Can't ask for nothin' else," the man replied.

"Boy...you suppose a man could take a *copper* for a run in a piece 'uh garbage like that?" one man spoke up, pointing behind a shop at the side of the building.

From where I stood I could only see the tail end of the car. As I looked back at the men and scanned the group of faces, standing right beside me was the man who was driving the car in lead of the police just a few hours before; the same man who appeared to be telling a story as Lucky and I approached the store.

As he and I locked eyes once again, he winked at me, smiling with that same smile he had shown me as he sped by.

"I suppose so, sir, suppose he jus might...if he quick enough," I answered, clutching my suitcase and rod.

"Ah c'mon, he ain't got no idea what he talkin' about!" one man blurted out, waving his hand in the air to dismiss my comment as they all chimed in, laughing.

"Told you, boys, I ain't got no time in tellin' stories...I outran that copper; even the boy in belief," the man spoke up, patting me on the back which forced me to take a step forward.

Lucky sat still at my side while I remained in one spot, watching keenly as the men continued to laugh and prod at the one who'd stated his claim.

"Bet if that copper come through here now, you boys sure be quick to cut that out," he spoke up in an effort to silence the group.

"Should I jus tell 'em I seen you do it?" I questioned softly, looking up at the man as the others laughed.

"It ain't gonna make no difference, they already got their minds made up that it ain't possible," he replied. You wanna soda?" he asked, smiling.

"Sure, sir, please, yes please," I replied with a smile.

"C'mon inside," he suggested.

"What about my dog, sir?" I asked, looking down at Lucky.

"He'll be fine," he answered, gesturing toward the group of men.

The group's laughing slowed as we walked away and their attention turned to Lucky, petting and praising him.

I walked alongside the man into the store and stood at the counter with him as he paid for two sodas.

"Here yah go...." he started.

"Poor Boy, sir, my name's Poor Boy," I stated as I gripped the cool bottle of pop.

"Well, Poor Boy, it's nice to meet 'cha," he said as he tapped his bottle against mine.

"Thank you, sir, uh..." I replied, smiling.

"Name's Amos," he stated. "And you can cut it out with all that *sir* nonsense, I ain't but twenty," he added, opening the door to exit the store.

He sat down on the edge of the platform outside the storefront. I looked over at Lucky to see that he was more than content with being the center of attention, and I joined Amos at his side.

"What's with the suitcase?" he asked, looking over at it as I set it down at my side.

"Jus takin' a little trip," I replied simply.

"Oh yeah, where to?" he prodded with a gentle laugh.

"Lookin' to find me some miracles," I answered, squinting against the sun which was at his back.

"Miracles?" he asked.

"Yes," I replied quickly, nodding my head.

"What sorta miracles you got in mind?" he followed up, taking a swill of his soda.

"Not sure...imagine I'll know when I see 'em," I said, looking up at the sky.

"I imagine you will," he replied with encouragement.

We sat quietly for a few minutes, neither of us saying a word, just staring off into the field across the road.

"What was you runnin' from...back there on the road?" I blurted out, breaking the silence.

"Can't say I was runnin' from anything," he replied, smiling. "You don't have nobody that's gonna be worried about you?" he asked softly.

"I left a note," I stated.

He soon got up and walked toward the group of young men, who all remained in pretty much the same positions as we'd left them; Lucky was at the center of them, still enjoying the spotlight.

Amos centered himself in the group of men and rubbed Lucky's belly while he smart mouthed a few of them. They all seemed to share quite a bond in humor, and none of them appeared to take it to heart what the other was saying; it wasn't something I'd ever witnessed before. I smiled as I watched and listened, anticipating what was going to be said next.

One of the men asked me what I was doing with a suitcase and where I was headed. When I replied in the same manner I'd done with Amos, the man laughed at me. Another joined in on the laughter for a brief moment, right before Amos stood up and slapped him across the face. Everything went quiet.

"It's okay, I been laughed at before," I explained quietly as I put my hands up.

"No, it ain't okay," Amos replied, not taking his eyes off the man who first began laughing. "Apologize to my young friend," Amos demanded.

"Man, you're crazy, he jus a kid...I ain't sayin' sorry to no kid," the man replied, waving his hand in the air.

"Poor Boy, you ready for your first miracle?" Amos asked, looking down at me.

"Not too sure, Amos, sir," I answered, weary of what was about to happen.

"Now what I tell you about them *sirs*?" he questioned, smiling at me.

"Right," I replied simply.

"Poor Boy...you figure a man got much chance walkin' anywhere with two broken legs?" Amos inquired with this tone of complete confidence.

"Don't figure so, no," I answered, unsure of what to say.

"How 'bout after he been dragged behind a car; what kinda chance you figure he got in breathing proper with busted up ribs?" he asked calmly.

The man remained straight faced while the others still hadn't opened their mouths to interfere in any sort of way; bring peace, resolution, or anything.

"Not too good, I imagine," I replied as I clutched my suitcase and rod in preparation to run.

"Boy, I ain't mean nothin' by it," the man spoke up.

I looked at Amos.

"You good with that?" Amos asked of me.

"I'm good," I answered, nodding my head.

"Let's get outta here," Amos suggested as he patted me on the shoulder, leading me toward his car.

Lucky was quick to follow.

"You getting in or you jus gonna stand there?" Amos asked as we reached his car and I stood still at its side.

"I ain't never been nowhere with someone I ain't shared a meal with," I replied, scratching my arm.

"Gonna make you feel any better if I get you a burger?" he asked, smiling, playfully annoyed.

"Jus might," I answered plainly.

"Anyone ever tell you that you a bit of a pain?" he questioned as he smacked the roof of his car, expelling a small cloud of settled dust.

"A time or two," I replied, looking down at Lucky.

I stayed a couple of steps behind him as we walked back toward the front of the store. Passing the group of guys that hadn't yet changed their positions, Amos made a point to stop for a brief moment and gently cup the side of the man's face who he'd slapped, and then playfully rubbed his hair as he told him, *"I love you"*, just once. The other men remained quiet as the moment occurred, as did I, still in one spot, while the man looked up at Amos from where he sat and softly responded, *"I love you too"*.

As I looked around at the others I noticed each of them take a moment to themselves to slowly drop their head and smile.

"Let's get you that burger," Amos said as he turned to me before heading toward the store.

There was a small diner attached to the store, which Amos led me into.

The serving staff was made up of young women in uniforms, while there was a man behind a small hole in the wall who appeared to be the cook. He was scruffy looking, wearing a small white hat, and from the moment we entered he was shouting and smacking his hand over a small bell on the countertop, which was at the edge of his hole in the wall; I'd never seen anything like it. The girls wouldn't take their eyes off of Amos as we found our seat. They were staring and giggling, nudging each other to have a look. He walked in a way that commanded notice but it wasn't with any arrogance, it was something else; maybe just who he was.

"You happy here?" a girl asked as we sat down.

"Yes, thank you," Amos replied, smiling.

"Can I get you something to drink?" she asked, not taking her eyes off of Amos.

"Sure 'uh, I dunno...you wanna shake?" he asked, nodding his head just once as he turned to look at me.

"Shake?" I replied, confused.

"Yeah...you like chocolate?" he questioned, laughing.

"Chocolate?" I asked.

"Just bring us two chocolate shakes 'n one cheeseburger," he said to the waitress as he flicked his fingers, using two and then one.

"You do know what cheese is though, right?" he teased, chuckling.

"I believe so, yes," I replied, smiling.

"So, tell me more about these miracles you in search of," he suggested as he crossed his arms, resting them on the table.

"Why'd you tell that man you love him?" I asked as I sat on my hands, leaning against the table.

"'Cause I do," he replied simply.

"He somebody to you?" I questioned, curiously.

"Does he need to be?" he asked without any hesitation.

"I dunno...guess not," I replied, shrugging my shoulders.

The waitress soon brought us our order. Once I found a moment to taste the chocolate milkshake, after staring at it until Amos explained what it was, I couldn't be bothered to speak again until I was finished. I'd never had anything so amazing swirl around in my mouth. Amos watched with a smile as, with great enjoyment, I worked my way between the milkshake and burger until they were both done.

As I wiped my face with a napkin that Amos handed to me, I thought of Hope and how much she would have enjoyed sharing in such a treat. I smiled thinking of her and was uplifted as I was reminded of my mission at hand.

"You figure you full 'n able to take a ride now?" he asked, smacking his hand down on the table.

I nodded my head, smiling, as I took one last look around.

Lucky was awaiting our return as we made our way down the few steps onto the gravel, outside the diner. The group of men had all gone, leaving Lucky to lay against the wall in the hot sun. There was a hose out back, as we neared the car, and Amos stopped to fill up a small dish he'd found on the ground for Lucky to have a drink from. I filled my hands and splashed my face as Amos held the hose, and then I did the same for him. Once Lucky lapped up the water we were on our way.

His car seemed to have a tough time starting as he spoke softly to it while cranking over the engine. Lucky sat still in the backseat as I sat in the front, peering over the dash out the front window.

"C'mon, c'mon, I know you're in there...jus for me, like you do," he spoke under his breath, pumping the gas pedal vigorously with his foot.

I looked back at Lucky, snickering, as I'd never heard such a thing; a man whispering to a vehicle.

It started. He rubbed the dash with gratitude, praising the car as he slowly revved the engine and then let off so it could idle. Amos looked over at me, smiling, then winked just once.

"Just gotta let 'er know you love her," he explained in a soft tone.

"Her?" I asked, confused.

"You'll get it one day," he replied, smacking me on the thigh.

He put the car in drive and off we went. There was a crackling sound coming from the top of the dash as dust poured in from the floor. Amos reached over me and rolled down the window.

"It'll get better once we get moving," he insisted, smiling.

I simply nodded my head as I let out a cough, covering my mouth.

I assumed he was speaking of the speed at which we were traveling but it seemed as though we were already moving quite fast, and I thought that was the root of why so much dust was entering the car.

I rested my arm up on the door, leaving my hand hanging outside the car to deflect some fresh air in my direction. Bug after bug hitting my open hand I almost retreated but it was well worth it as I was soon relieved of the excess dust working to fill my lungs.

"You gonna make it?" Amos asked loudly as he looked over at me.

I nodded my head, squinting through the haze, as I smiled with uncertainty.

As the dust cleared, I watched the world pass by at a speed I'd never experienced before. Every few minutes I'd look over at Amos and then into the backseat at Lucky just to bring myself back to reality; I loved it.

The crackling from the speakers soon turned to a choppy version of music and little breaks of talking. It didn't seem to bother Amos as he appeared to be in his own world, so I followed his lead and remained in mine.

After driving in what seemed to be the opposite direction of home for some time, Amos turned off the road we were on and headed down a narrow trail into the woods. A strange feeling came over me as, for the first time in my life, I was completely unsure of where I was, and I'd never been so aware of that. I didn't want to bring any attention to my concern or feelings of discomfort as I was still unclear on where we were going. Nervously, I sat still.

"You ready?" Amos asked as he flicked the car up into neutral and turned the engine off, leaving us to roll freely.

"Ready?" I asked, propping myself up in my seat.

"Bring that dog 'uh yours up front," he insisted, smiling, as he continued to steer the rolling car.

"C'mon boy," I summoned Lucky, slapping my lap, looking to the backseat.

As we neared an opening on the trail, Amos instructed me to open my door and prepare to jump.

"Huh?" I asked, confused.

Before I could finish with a follow up, questioning his mental state, he had already leaped from the moving car.

"Jump!" he yelped as he hit the ground.

I peered over the dash only to see that I was quickly approaching a large body of water.

"Jump!" I heard once more.

With no time to think I flung open the car door, held it propped open with my foot as I coaxed Lucky to leap, and then I did the same.

As I smacked the ground and rolled a few times I could hear the car hit the water and just as it did, Amos let out a loud howl.

"You okay?" he questioned as I came to a stop, lying on my stomach.

I looked up. *"You nuts?"* I belted, slowly making my way to my feet as I scanned the trail for Lucky.

"That wake you up?" he teased as he bent over, placing his hands on his knees.

"I wasn't sleepin'," I replied, uncertain of his approach.

He laughed.

"Lucky!" I shouted, looking around.

Lucky made his way out of the trees with a newfound look of distrust on his face. He wasn't pleased and understandably so, I'd just tossed him from a moving car.

"What would make you wanna do somethin' like that?" I asked of Amos as Lucky slowly neared my side.

"Wasn't mine to begin with, and it won't be long before we get sought out," he explained, kneeling down to pet Lucky.

He continued to pet Lucky, speaking softly to him, as I stared at the car which was now only visible by the trunk poking out of the water. My concern was growing for how I was going to find my way back home or what I might say if the police were to find me in the company of Amos and what sounded like a car that didn't belong to him.

"You in some kinda trouble?" I asked, scratching my elbow as I turned to look at him.

"No more than the next man," he replied simply, still petting Lucky, not skipping a beat.

"What now?" I asked of him as I stood, looking around.

"Follow me," he suggested, standing to his feet as he began to walk.

He started walking down a path through the woods to the left of where the car sat, submerged. I stared at the car as I thought of Hope and my uncertainty of how she was doing or how far I was from home. I shook my head, looked down at Lucky and continued to walk, keeping my pace a few steps behind Amos.

CHAPTER 13

After walking for what seemed like forever, with almost no speaking to one another, we came to a large clearing in the woods just as the sun was going down. There was a small house with a single lantern burning off to the right side of the front door. It didn't appear to have anyone inside as we approached with it being quite dark within. I could hear rustling in behind the house as the air was still and night was falling upon the woods. My curiosity was growing, yet I didn't speak while we continued to near the house. Gaining in on what seemed to be our destination, a clear sound made its way into the air; I'd never heard anything like it. As the noise repeated itself, in the breaks of sound, was the mooing of a cow.

Instead of going to the front door, Amos led the way around to the back of the house. Just as we rounded the corner of the house I could see a lantern swinging in the air, being held in the hand of someone.

"Who's that?" I whispered softly as I sped up to get behind Amos.

"Who's there?" a voice shouted out from behind the lantern.

"It's me, grandpa...and I've come with a friend," Amos replied gently.

"Aaammoosss...." the man spoke slowly.

"Yes, grandpa, it's me," Amos replied with care.

Lucky made his way over to the animals to sniff them out.

"He okay, sir, he ain't no bother," I spoke up as the man lowered his lantern to have a look at Lucky approaching.

There was a small looking horse, which appeared to be the source of noise that I was strange to, tied to a tree with a long and ragged stretch of rope. As it let out another few quick rants, the old man belted at it to keep quiet; speaking to it as though they'd been burdened by each other for quite some time. A single cow roamed around, slowly, as we stood in our tracks, with Amos and his grandfather making small talk. I didn't pay much attention to what was being said as I was rather caught up in my surroundings.

The old man held the lantern up near Amos' face as they spoke to one another. I caught myself staring at him as I was trying to figure out what he had draped over his upper body. It appeared to be a thin, wool blanket with a hole cut out for his head, while his legs were bare and he had on a pair of boots and a large hat pulled down low, leaving little light to see his face. He was hunched over, seemingly weathered from life as he stood in what I'd guess as being a seventy-year-old body.

The horse seemed to be annoyed by Lucky and it once again let out a loud noise. The man turned, swinging his lantern to have a better look, just as I called Lucky to my side.

"Sound like your horse got a cold, sir," I suggested.

"That ain't no horse, boy, that there's a donkey...*a jackass,*" he replied, scoffing at his animal.

I simply shrugged my shoulders as I quietly repeated his words to myself. I'd never seen or heard of such an animal before but it sure appeared to know its way around the old mans' nerves.

There was almost no daylight left in the woods as we stood out behind the house, while Amos and his grandfather continued to visit. Soon, one after the other, following his grandfathers' lead, we made our way to the front entrance of the house. Lucky was asked to wait outside; which he did, lying down on the front porch out-side the door.

Once we entered the house the old man ordered me to go collect some wood from the pile outside, instructing me to use the lantern hanging on the porch as my source of light. I did as I was asked, and soon returned from the woodpile with all that I could grab.

"Put it down there," he demanded, with only the dim light from his single lantern lighting up the space of his home.

"Here, sir?" I asked, uncertain.

"That'll do," he replied sharply.

I couldn't place Amos anywhere in the house for all that I could see, nor could I hear his voice.

"Make us a fire," the old man continued with his orders.

"Yes sir," I replied simply as my comfort level was declining at a fast pace.

"Anything in particular you'd like to be called?" he asked as I kneeled down to begin making a fire.

"Poor Boy, sir...my name 'uh, it, it's Poor Boy," I replied, standing to my feet to introduce myself.

"I bet it is," he suggested with a dry tone.

"Where'd Amos get off to?" I asked as I returned to my knees, building the fire.

"I ain't seen that boy since god knows when, and there ain't no telling when I'll see him again," he answered from across the room as he shuffled around.

"Sir?" I questioned as a sense of fear rushed through me.

He didn't respond.

As I started to deal with thoughts of panic and uncertainty, while the old man had stopped shuffling around, I took a few deep breaths and worked on getting the fire going so I could at least gain a better understanding of my surroundings within the house.

With a short handled, small headed axe, I was quick to chip away at a single log as I kneeled down on the floor, working to create enough kindling to get the fire started in no time.

As the flame grew I added more wood and soon enough the light from the fire danced across the open space.

"Got it!" a voice rang out as the door flung open.

I turned to see as I stood to my feet; it was Amos.

My entire body let loose as a sigh of relief came over me.

"Got what?" I asked, excited to see him.

"Your suitcase...you left your suitcase in the...." he started, gripping my suitcase with both hands as he looked around.

I shrugged my shoulders and shook my head as he looked back at me, as if to clarify where his grandfather had gone.

"Grandpa, you in here?" Amos spoke out in question as he set my suitcase down and walked throughout the small house, checking each room.

He didn't return for a few minutes so as I waited I grabbed my suitcase and opened it in front of the fireplace. Everything remained as it was and none of it was so much as even the slightest bit damp. I laughed to myself as I thought of how welcoming the day had been, even in its many moments of uncertainty.

"What's so funny?" Amos asked as he entered the room.

"Thank you for gettin' this...I thought you..." I started, looking up at Amos.

"Thought I what...left you here...with **him**?" he asked, smiling down at me.

"Well, it's jus that..." I went on, feeling ashamed.

"Just what?" he questioned, concerned, as he knelt down to meet me.

"Thank you...thank you is all," I insisted, smiling.

"You hungry?" he asked, patting me on the shoulder as he stood to his feet. "He's *lights out* in the next room, bet he won't wake 'till the sun comes up," he explained as he started to root through the cupboards.

Amos cooked up some eggs while I sliced a few pieces of hard crusted bread for each of us to lather in butter, as we sat and ate in the flickering light of the fire, sharing in each others' company yet again.

Once we were done eating, Amos asked me to join him outside while he puffed on his grandfathers' pipe. Lucky snuggled his way in between us as we sat down on the edge of the porch steps. Amos explained that he didn't smoke very often but any chance he had to sneak in some time with that pipe, he did just that. He said that it was magical, that there was just something about it, which he attributed to his grandfathers' travelling. Amos was so well intended with his words that I could feel what he was saying as I hung on to every last one. As he extended an offering for me to taste the travels of an old man within the simple puff of some pipe tobacco, I too did just that. I also had some lingering curiosity of my own from time spent around Mr. Charlie and his pipe.

Trying to play it cool, I closed my eyes as my mouth and then lungs filled with smoke; but before I could lose myself in the magic which I sought, I began to cough like never before.

Lucky jumped to his feet, as did I, dropping the pipe on the ground while Amos worked to contain his laughter. Amos rapidly tapped me on the leg, as I was still coughing, in an effort to gain my attention. Once I managed to stop coughing I opened my eyes, clearing away the tears with my hands, only to see the bright light of a lantern just inches away from my face; it was the old man.

"Might I bother you to suggest that you go die on someone else's front porch?" the man spoke in a dry tone as he brought his face into the light of his burning lantern, just inches away from mine.

"No need, sir, I'm done," I replied as I let out one last cough and gasp for air.

Amos laughed.

"I can't find my pipe," the old man stated.

"Right here, grandpa...it's here," Amos said as he handed it to him.

"Funny...I don't remember leaving it in your hands," his grand-father grumbled.

"We had a bite, grandpa...while you were asleep, we made us a bite to eat," Amos spoke without caution.

"I wasn't sleeping...and I ain't no fool, I know you fixed a bite, I could hear the two 'uh you snoopin' around in there," he interrupted Amos.

I knelt down to pet Lucky as I was feeling uncomfortable and didn't quite know what else to do.

"Did you want us to put something together for you...to eat?" Amos asked, looking up from where he sat.

"I'll fix my own food, same as I been doin' since long before you came along...*you and your friend here*," his grandpa snapped back.

"Okay grandpa, I'll leave you to it," Amos replied with ease as he stood to his feet.

"Might need some more 'uh that wood," I suggested to Amos.

"Good idea," he returned, leading us off the porch.

With Lucky quickly trailing behind, most likely in an effort to escape the energy on the porch, we made our way to the woodpile.

Amos didn't say a single word about his grandfather, nor did I bring it up. I knew what it was like to be around that type of person and I just figured there was no sense in bringing any extra attention to it, especially if Amos didn't feel the need.

Standing under the bright light of the full moon, Amos joked around as he piled wood upon my arms. He continued to push his luck, trying to add just one too many pieces onto my load, and each time he did I'd drop them all; we'd have a laugh then he'd start all over again. This went on much longer than it should have but I think we were both in need of some laughter after the long day we'd had.

With a load of wood weighing down my arms as they were stretched out in front of me, and Amos with both of his arms full as he'd managed to grab two small stacks, we made our way back to the house.

I could smell the aroma of his grandfathers' pipe as we approached the backside of the house. The donkey appeared to be sleeping as he stood still in one spot, just a few feet from the tree where he was tied. Lucky made an attempt to veer off track and pay a visit but I quietly urged him back to my side before he could do so. With the sky clear and the moon full it was as bright as early morning, being so far in the bush.

"Never had a thought I was lucky before but, now...I *know* I ain't," his grandfather grumbled as we made our way up the porch.

"Somethin' the matter?" Amos questioned him, stopping to do so.

"Thought maybe the two 'uh you got lost," the old man replied, exhaling a large puff of smoke as he sat in the shadow of light from the burning lantern.

"Ain't no such luck, grandpa," Amos said as he swung open the screen door with his fingertips, trying not to drop any wood.

Amos propped open the door with his foot until I made my way inside and then he let it slam shut on its springs behind him.

We stacked the wood next to the fireplace and then Amos went to get some blankets out for the two of us. He made a bed on the floor for himself while he insisted that I sleep on the couch. I was fine to spend the night on the floor but he planned otherwise.

"You gonna bleed out, boy, if you don't get that looked at," his grandfather said as he came into the house a few minutes later, grumbling, then went straight to his room in the back of the house.

"Your arm," Amos said with concern, pointing.

I looked down at my arm and the bandaging that Ms. Violet put on over the stitching was soaked in blood and had worked its way through my shirt sleeve. Between leaping from a vehicle in motion and stacking logs across my arms, somewhere along the way it must have torn my stitches.

"Sorry 'bout this," I said quietly as I looked up at Amos.

"Don't apologize for nothin'...take that shirt off 'n let me have a look," he replied with care.

"Wonder how he saw this?" I questioned, speaking of his grand-father.

"He don't miss a thing, believe in that," he said in return without skipping a beat.

Amos stepped outside for a moment to grab the lantern, which was still burning, hanging on the porch, and he brought it inside. Setting it on the kitchen table, he had me sit down while he put some water on to boil over the fire and got together a needle, thread, and fresh bandaging.

"How'd you manage this?" he asked as he slowly peeled off the bloody bandage.

"Was jus helpin' a friend," I replied, scrunching my face in pain.

"Sorry, sorry, it's *alllmoosst* off," he said as he peeled the last of it off. "So 'uh, this friend, they have anything to do with this journey you on?" he asked as he stood up to get the water off the fire.

"Think this gonna need a new stitch?" I asked, looking down at my arm.

"Don't know...let's clean it up 'n have a look," he replied, smiling, as he poured the boiling water into a basin on the table.

Amos took his time and gently scrubbed my arm, rinsing and washing it until it was clean. Thankfully, no stitches broke so he dabbed it dry then put a clean bandage around my arm as he apologized for forcing me to jump out of a moving car. I laughed and played it off but I was thankful for him acknowledging it.

After we cleaned up we got into our beds and talked about nothing in particular, in the flickering light of the fire, for a short time until he fell asleep; I followed suit shortly after.

I awoke in a panic, sitting up and unclear of how long I'd been asleep, I was drenched in sweat and found myself crying out for my grandmother. I managed to startle Amos enough that he woke soon after.

"What's wrong?" he asked with concern, quickly sitting up to look at me.

I couldn't find any words; I simply sat up, still under my blanket that I'd been given to sleep with, and I sobbed. Amos sat down next to me on the edge of the couch and rubbed my back, not asking another question of me.

Suddenly, I missed everything; I missed my grandmother, I missed Ms. Violet, Mr. Charlie, I missed Hope, and most of all, I just missed home. This was all new to me; I'd never been away from everything that was familiar to me, especially all at once. As I found a moment of clarity I made my way, just a few feet from where I was, over to my suitcase; I flung it open, grabbed my grandmothers' bottle of perfume, and I sprayed both of my wrists. I climbed back under my blanket, kept my hands tucked under my nose and I watched the fire, without saying a single word. Amos didn't flinch through any of it, he just watched me for a few minutes and then crawled back into his bed on the floor. He smiled at me as I was overcome with calmness from the scent of my grandmothers' perfume.

I continued to watch the fire as Amos added more wood to its need and then I slowly dozed off, opening my eyes each time I fell asleep, until I was out.

I woke the next morning to the clanging of dishes in the kitchen. With my hands still in place under my nose, I opened my eyes and slowly looked around, connecting to my surroundings.

"You sure smell pretty," the old man belted as he bent over looking at me, bringing his face just inches away from mine.

From my point of view he appeared upside down, because I was on my back, but it was nice to finally see his face in its entirety. He had a big smile, staring into my eyes as he tilted his head, cockeyed, playfully closing one eye, and then the other.

"My grandmothers' perfume, sir...that'd be what 'chu smell," I replied as I stared up at him.

"*I **like** it*," he said with enthusiasm, raising his eyebrows.

"Thank you, sir" I replied, unsure of his behavior.

"Eggs'll do?" he blurted out.

"Sir?" I questioned.

"*Good enough*...make your way over when you good 'n ready," he yelped as he stood up straight, tapping me on the forehead with a spoon and then turning to walk away.

I laid still on the couch for a few minutes, collecting myself, as I became curious about where Amos was at, seeing that he wasn't on the floor where I'd last seen him.

"*Wheeew!*" Amos belted as he entered the house.

I quickly sat up to look over the back of the couch.

"Where'd you get off to?" I asked of him, curiously.

"You mind?" his grandfather spoke out as he flicked his hand, pointing to the open door.

"Best way to start the day is a cold morning swim," Amos said as he swung his leg out behind him, kicking the door shut. "Ain't that right, grandpa?" he asked playfully as he patted me on the head.

"C'mon, sit down," his grandfather ordered.

"You okay?" Amos asked of me as he knelt down over the back of the couch.

I simply nodded my head then stood to my feet and began folding up the blankets I had used.

Amos and his grandfather both sat down at the table, one at either end, and watched me as I neatly stacked the blankets at the foot of the couch.

"This a fine young man you brought us here," his grandfather said to Amos, teasing.

"Would seem that way," Amos replied, smiling, rubbing his hands together.

"Come, c'mon, I think you got 'em," his grandfather insisted.

"Yes sir," I replied as I made my way to the table.

"I look like someone who have any interest in bein' called such a thing?" his grandfather asked of me.

"*Do I?*" Amos belted. "He was doin' the same thing to me," he finished, laughing, as I sat down.

"What might you suggest?" I inquired softly.

"Otis...the only name my beautiful momma gave me," he suggested, smiling, as he scraped the pan over my plate, filling it with scrambled eggs.

I smiled as I waited my turn to begin eating.

The three of us sat and ate, visiting, until all of the food which Otis had cooked was gone.

Throughout the meal I was stricken by brief moments of missing everyone back home; the morning, the time at the table eating; it all had such similarities to how we spent our mornings with each other at home that it brought about this rush of emotion, swooping in, visiting for a moment, and then leaving me. The newly realized sensation occurred, off and on, for most of the meal.

Amos and I cleaned up and did the dishes while Otis went outside onto the porch to smoke his pipe.

As the smell of Otis' burning pipe came through the screen door on the front of the house, Amos continued to extend our time cleaning up as he whipped me with his towel and splashed me with water, creating a mess on the floor. I was always up for goofing around but somehow in this unfamiliar environment, I was hesitant and feeling off balance. I could see that Amos was making an effort to ease my mind, I was just having a hard time allowing myself the freedom to do so.

Once we finally finished cleaning up we joined Otis on the front porch.

"So jus what brings you here anyway, Poor Boy?" Otis asked me as I sat down on the step next to Lucky.

"I come here with him, with Amos" I replied, looking over at Amos.

"I know *how* you got here...I mean what *brought* you here; ain't 'chu got a home or some people who's gonna be missin' you?" he questioned, exhaling a large cloud of smoke.

"Miracles, grandpa...he's in search 'uh miracles," Amos spoke up, nodding his head as he winked at me.

"*Miracles*...that true?" Otis asked, leaning forward in his seat as he closed one eye to avoid it being filled with smoke.

I sat still, unsure of how to respond for fear of being ridiculed.

"*Well?*" Otis blurted out.

"Yes sir," I replied as I sat nervously, petting Lucky.

"*Poor Boy, out lookin' for miracles...well ain't that jus somethin' straight out 'uh poem*," Otis suggested, looking out beyond the porch.

I lowered my head, looking down at Lucky as I continued to claw at clumps of fur that had formed in his coat.

"What is it you runnin' from?" he asked. "'Cause you runnin' from somethin', or you wouldn't be sittin' here on my porch," he finished, sitting back in his chair.

"Sir?" I asked, unsure of his intention.

"It's Otis," he demanded simply. "Now what on earth would give a boy your age the notion to go out searchin' for miracles?" he asked. "Somethin's gotta have you runnin'," he suggested softly.

"My friend, Hope...she sick," I replied simply.

"Hmmm," he mumbled, breathing heavily out of his nose, biting down on his pipe.

"She been sick a while?" Amos asked gently.

"Don't know...she took a spell when we was out in the woods and she ain't woke up since," I explained as Otis packed the smoking ashes in his pipe with his thumb.

"And jus who was it that put you on to miracles?" Otis jumped in.

"Ms. Violet said to keep an eye out, and I jus figured why wait for 'em if I can go find 'em," I explained with confidence.

"Jus what exactly you think a miracle is, that have you figure you can jus set out and find 'em like that?" Otis questioned me.

"Can't say, really, but, if Ms. Violet says they out there then I gotta believe in that, and jus hope I know when the time is right," I said, stroking Lucky as he looked up at me with the mentioning of Ms. Violet.

"And you got yourself a feeling that you on the right track?" Otis prodded.

"Why was you so miserable when we come in last night?" I returned, stopping my petting of Lucky as I looked up at Otis.

Otis sat back in his chair as it appeared that I had caught him off guard. He stared at me, silently, while he continued to puff deeply on his pipe, losing his rhythm as he blew out some tobacco.

Amos seemed to have been relaxed by my question, as though it maybe took some pressure off of him to pretend Otis wasn't miserable.

"You like being here...eating, drinking, sleeping...the door open to all your needs for no cost 'uh nothing?" Otis replied sharply as he leaned forward to make eye contact with me.

"You been real kind in that sense, sir, Otis...but I been not wanted for long stretches 'uh my short life, and if I'm a bother, or my friend bein' sick is a bother to hear about, same as my seekin' out miracles, jus say the word and I'll have my back to you," I said sternly, pointing toward the bush.

I could see Amos out of the corner of my eye, smiling and nodding his head as I spoke.

As fast I had reacted and spoke up I wanted to fix it with an apology, but I knew what I was feeling was right and I'd never spoke up for myself before, not like that. It felt good, so I ignored the pondering of my mind to say sorry.

Once I decided that I wasn't going to apologize I sat up just a little bit straighter and watched Otis for his response, although he didn't say anything; he simply winked at me and nodded his head just once.

Otis stood to his feet and asked Amos and myself to join him behind the house to help feed the animals.

The three of us joked with each other as we took turns grabbing handfuls of grain from a bucket to spread out for the chickens and laying hens. There was a pen further into the bush that housed some pigs, which we also went to feed.

Arriving near dark the evening before, I missed noticing most of what Otis had behind the house. There was another cow and one bull; both of which were roaming around freely along with the initial one I'd seen when we came in. The donkey was still tied to the tree and it appeared to have frayed the rope even more than it already was. Otis hollered at it to stop chewing on the rope, which made Amos and I laugh and encouraged the donkey to belt back as it seemed to be annoyed, yet again.

"That little sshh...he ain't gonna stop 'till he gets what he wants...and I'm runnin' outta rope," Otis shouted as he went off into the bush.

Amos and I looked at each other, laughing, as we could hear Otis still grumbling and stomping around in the bush, sounding to be breaking branches.

One of the cows slowly made its way over to us, then Amos started to run his hand over its back and as he did its tail started to flip back and forth, smacking me in the face. I started to laugh and I caught its tail right inside my mouth just as I inhaled, leading me to laugh uncontrollably; and then of course Lucky ran over and nipped at the heel of the cow, scaring it away. Amos and I couldn't stop laughing until he pointed at Otis coming out of the bush.

"This gonna keep you quiet?" he asked, speaking to the donkey as he dragged behind him a long branch.

Otis began to massage the donkey, as he spoke softly to it, with a sequence of different strokes and a light whipping method; which was seemingly something that had to have been a routine of some sort.

Amos simply shook his head and laughed as we turned to go chop wood.

"So what's 'ur plan?" Amos asked of me as we walked, side by side.

"Plan?" I replied, looking up at him.

"Well, you wanna just take it as it comes and keep an eye out from here...with me?" he questioned, encouragingly.

I got the feeling that he was concerned for me and didn't want to upset me so his approach was quite light, and ultimately, leaving it up to me. When I set out the day before I didn't have any plan in mind on how long I'd need or be gone, so I was becoming at ease and in fact relieved that I had made a friend so quickly; and one who was open to meeting me with choices and understanding.

"Yeah, that sound jus fine by me," I replied, smiling. "Otis gonna be okay with that?" I asked, playfully uncertain.

"He'll be fine...it would seem like you done put him in his place any-way...it's good for him," he said, laughing, as he cupped the back of my head with his hand.

"I ain't mean nothin' by that, I jus..." I started.

"You ain't gotta explain yourself to me...I know, I know how it is, and I think it's a good thing to speak up when you feel you ain't bein' treated fair," he explained, stopping to look at me.

I smiled as we stood still for a moment, and then Amos kicked up his leg to hit me in the behind; lunging forward, I laughed, as we went on to grab an axe and made our way into the bush to collect some wood.

Amos pushed over any smaller dead trees that stood awaiting the wind as I started to pile some deadfall.

Getting to know each other, we shared in stories about our lives, as well as some trivial small talk. I talked about my upbringing and my grandmother, Ms. Violet, Mr. Charlie, and I spoke about Hope and how different my life had been since she came into it; since her being my first ever real friend. He told me about him losing his mother to illness and his father dying soon after his mothers' death. He explained that his grandfather (Otis) had turned into a recluse, seeking refuge in the woods after his wife (Amos' grandmother) had died; but he said that Otis seemed to have gotten worse since his daughter (Amos' mom) passed away. Amos went on to say that his parents died when he was around what appeared to be my age, and he'd been coming and going, walking his own path, making a life of his own, ever since. He said that he checks in on his grand-father for short periods of time every now and again, whenever he gets the notion to do so.

As time passed while we chopped wood and visited, without breaks, I was feeling better about my decision to stay. I wasn't sure how long I'd stick around but for as much as I was missing home and wanted to get back to see Hope and wondered how she was doing, I felt like being where I was would better serve the journey I set out on.

Amos and I walked back to the house and grabbed a sheet of plywood, which Otis had constructed for himself, with two holes in either corner of one end and a rope strung through for pulling. As the grass and small brush was quite lush where we had to go back to for the wood, I sat on the plywood while Amos pulled, which led me to, essentially, float across the ground.

We didn't skip a beat in our back and forth as we stacked the wood we had gathered and chopped onto the sheet of plywood, before slowly making our way back toward the house. Even with just getting to know each other and with the difference in our age, we were like old pals. He was very generous with his time and interest in listening and yet still very playful; much like what an older brother would be I guess, had I been introduced to such a thing any earlier in life.

Just as we finished stacking the wood, Otis stepped out onto the front porch, with us in clear sight, and began to smack a spoon against a pan, shouting at us to come in for lunch. It was something that he clearly just wanted to do, rather than any real need to gain our attention.

There was a small washbasin just outside the front door, sitting on a wooden stool, with a steel jug filled with cold water at its side. Amos washed up first and I followed, then we went inside to eat.

Between breakfast and now lunch, it was quite apparent that Otis didn't mess around in the kitchen. Everything was fresh and cooked with great attention and care; much like Ms. Violet and her approach to feeding her loved ones. Once we were seated it was fair game at filling our bellies, but the intention and effort that went in to us being fed was very comforting.

The day continued with much of the same work: eating, visiting, laughter and then preparing for bed. The three of us sat on the front porch, drinking tea, not forcing any conversation, while Otis puffed on his pipe under the light of a single lantern.

I was the first to turn in as I wanted to have a moment alone to spray my grandmothers' perfume on myself before crawling under my blankets. Amos and Otis soon entered the house, with neither of them bringing any attention to the scent of perfume lingering in the air, and then we all said goodnight.

There was a rhythm to life that seemed to flow with a greater sense of ease when it was given the room to perform in its intention; and this was becoming all the more apparent as I tried to quiet my mind and just watch.

CHAPTER 14

I slept straight through the night and into the morning, without waking even once. That was the first time I'd experienced such a sleep for as long as I could remember.

I opened my eyes to the sound of a loud banging outside. As I laid on my back I scanned the room, before sitting up; Amos was still sleeping at my side, on the floor. I stood to my feet and went outside, onto the porch.

I could smell raw fuel and saw clouds of smoke billowing out from one of the buildings, where the source of noise seemed to be coming from.

As I walked barefoot down the steps and started out across the yard, out from the building came Otis; he was behind the wheel of a big, flatbed pickup truck. I couldn't tell what color it was because it was covered in bird droppings, and as a breeze picked up just as he pulled all the way out, a large cloud of dust blew off the cab and deck. He honked the horn just one time as he noticed me, once the smoke and dust cleared, then waved me over with a big smile on his face as he had one arm hanging outside the window.

After smacking the side of the cab with his hand he put the truck in park, opened the door from the outside, and then hopped out.

"She gave me some trouble...coughed a bit, tried to fight me off but, I ain't done with her jus yet," he spoke loudly over the sound of the engine.

I smiled, thinking of Amos and how he spoke to the car as he was trying to start it, just days before.

"Where's the boy?" Otis asked with his hands on his waist.

Just as we turned to look at the house, Amos came walking outside.

"You drive without pants, too?" Amos questioned Otis, taking note of his bare legs.

Otis was dressed the same as he had been since we first met: boots, a hat, and what appeared to be a blanket with a hole cut out for his head, draped over his upper body.

"Don't need but a pair 'uh hands and one quick foot," Otis replied, smiling, smacking his hands together.

"What's goin' on?" Amos asked, combing back his hair with his hand.

"Figured we'd go drag out that wreck you felt was trash enough to leave under water," Otis explained in short, looking down at me.

I just shrugged my shoulders and looked over at Amos.

"What wreck is that?" Amos questioned Otis, playing dumb.

"You tell me...heard you was tearin' around, and lo 'n behold you show up here on foot; meanwhile there's a car sittin' in water not a long mile from where we at," Otis replied, pointing down the clearing through the woods.

When we first left the car and walked to where we now stood, I could have sworn it was much further than just one mile.

"You say somethin'?" Amos asked, looking down at me as I stood between the two of them, with Lucky at my side.

With my lips sealed tightly against one another, I quickly shook my head.

"I saw for myself," Otis spoke up.

Amos cocked his head back in a show of uncertainty.

"Was out that way with the sun for some fish 'n caught a four-thousand-pound chunk 'uh steel that wasn't there three days ago...jus put it together," Otis explained without much care.

"You got chains on there?" Amos asked, looking on the deck of the truck.

"On the floor, in the cab," Otis replied, patting me on the back.

The three of us piled into the loud, still smoking large truck, and proceeded to where the car sat, submerged in the lake.

As I was squeezed in between the two of them on the torn up bench seat, I was at the mercy of the shifter ramming against my legs each time Otis changed gears; and each time he did, he followed with a quiet apology and a light tap on my leg.

The trail was quite bumpy, going over fallen trees and large rocks poking out from the earth, and if my legs weren't pinned against the seat by the stick shift I'd have most likely bounced onto the lap of Amos. None of us said anything more than we needed to, as hearing our own thoughts over the clanging and banging of the truck and engine was challenge enough.

Once we got to the lake, with Lucky right behind, Otis ordered us out of the truck and instructed Amos to grab the chains. Amos took the lead and went into the water to hook up the chains to the car while he told me to hold on at the other end until Otis backed up, and then I was to hook them up to the truck. I stood off to one side as Otis began to back up, with his arm across the back of the seat and him peering out the small back window of the cab. Amos kept bobbing below the waters' surface then would come back up for air and share a few curse words, as he was having trouble hooking the chains up to the car. Otis backed up and stopped just as the water reached halfway up the back tires, then held the brake and shouted at me to drop the chains and get into the water to help Amos. I was hesitant for a moment as I thought of my last experience in the water at the creek.

"What's the worry?" Otis shouted out his window.

I didn't want to get into it with him and have to find a way to explain that I was scared and couldn't swim.

"No worry!" I yelled back as I dropped the chains and slowly walked into the water.

Lucky started to bark and jump from side to side the further I walked in.

With my arms up in the air and me being in the water up to my waist, I started to breathe heavily as my mind began to race. I was balancing on the tips of my toes just as Amos came back up once again.

"You got it?" Otis bellowed from inside the cab of the truck.

Amos didn't reply, he just looked at me with concern.

"What are you doin' in here...you okay, you don't look too good, can you swim?" he rambled with concern.

I shook my head, shivering.

"Don't come no further, I just about got it, I'll get it this time...*myself...you stay there,*" he instructed me as he smiled, taking in a deep breath and then ducking below the waters' surface.

"He got it?" Otis questioned, yelling.

"Says this time," I replied, cupping my hands around my mouth as I took a few steps back.

Lucky was still barking, pouncing back and forth, side to side, at the waters' edge. He would take a step into the water and then quickly jump back, barking with such fury and seeming concern.

I stood still, shivering, but didn't want to get out of the water until Amos resurfaced and had the chains hooked up.

It felt like he was down there forever.

Otis honked the horn. I looked over at him as he flung one arm out the window and then caught eyes with me in the side mirror. I raised my hands in the air and then dropped them against the waters' surface, and just as I did, Amos popped back up.

"Got it!" he rejoiced, gasping for air as he gave a thumbs up.

Otis smacked his hand against the side of the truck and honked the horn, holding it down for a few seconds. I laughed.

Amos and I, side by side, left the water; and with him talking me through it, as he kneeled at my side, I hooked up the chains to the rear of the Otis' truck.

Otis put the truck in gear and slowly released the clutch as he gave it gas. As the slack pulled tight in the chains, the back tires on the truck started to grip and then slowly slip. Otis rolled back and tried again; same thing. He tried it a few more times but was slowly digging himself down, so he backed up further into the water and shouted at us to get out of the way.

Just as we got back a few steps into the tall grass and weeds at the waters' edge, Otis dropped the clutch and put the gas pedal to the floor. The engine screamed, Otis howled, the chains quickly lost slack at the sound of a loud thud in the air, and sure enough the car slowly crawled out from the water. Amos smacked his hand across my chest and we laughed, while Lucky barked from the other side of the truck, and Otis continued his howling within the cab as he pulled the car out the rest of the way. The car drained water from every seam and hole in its tired old body as it made its way out of the water and onto land, by the slow but steady pull from Otis.

"That's her!" Otis exclaimed as he stopped and hopped out of the truck.

I raised my eyebrows and laughed, shaking my head; with Otis being as upbeat and excitable as he was, it was infectious.

Amos and I stood next to each other, dripping wet and snickering, as Otis proceeded to inspect the car while he continued to praise himself and the job he'd just done retrieving it from the water.

"Dare I ask where this come from?" Otis asked of Amos as he stood up straight from the other side of the car.

"It's not like that, grandpa," Amos replied, standing still, clutching one hand in the other.

"Uh huh," Otis mumbled, looking at me.

"I jus jumped," I replied, shrugging my shoulders.

"That I believe," Otis said in return, winking at me.

Amos jumped up onto the deck of the truck and Otis got back into the cab after they both instructed me to get into the car and steer as it was being towed. I ensured them that I had no experience nor could I completely see over the dash but Otis insisted, as Amos encouraged it, and they gave me an old pair of boots from behind the seat of the truck to, *"either sit on 'em, or wear 'em to gain some length in reach of the brakes",* as Otis put it, before tossing them at me. I held the boots for a moment in one hand as I tried to think of which option was best, seeing no real benefit in either. I tossed them into the car, through the open window onto the seat, and opened the door to get in.

"How's that feel, feel good?" Amos shouted, smiling.

"Wet...feels wet," I replied under my breath, as the seat was soaking wet.

Amos gave me a thumbs up to question my being ready. Gripping the steering wheel with both hands, I relieved one and stuck it out the window to give a thumbs up in return; I was as ready as I thought I could be, under the circumstances.

"Hit it!" Amos shouted toward the cab, in the direction of Otis.

"What he say?" I questioned quietly to myself.

Before I could gather myself there was a loud bang and I jerked forward into the steering wheel; we were moving.

Otis honked the horn once and then began to pick up speed, just slightly.

Amos never took his eyes off of me as I bounced around in the car, working to press down on the brakes as needed when Otis had to slow for a fallen tree or curve in the trail. The brake pedal was very stiff and it didn't seem to help much no matter how hard I pressed. Thankfully, Otis was hitting every stump, fallen tree, rock and anything else he could, which seemed to do a good job at keeping me from smashing into the back of the truck.

By the time we pulled into the yard, my hands were cramping from gripping the steering wheel so tightly. Otis swung around near the shop so that I could stop in front of it. As I slid up and down on the seat to pump the brakes and do my best to look out the windshield, over the hood, I managed to stop where he intended for me to do so.

Amos leaped off the truck bed and ran over to open the door for me.

"You did it!" he belted with joy, holding the door open.

I grabbed a hold of the boots and dragged them across the seat then handed them to Amos; he laughed and patted me on the back.

"How'd that feel?" Otis bellowed as he approached the car to where Amos and I stood.

"Was good...but what, you couldn't find more trees or rocks to run over?" I teased.

Otis smacked Amos on the back and they both laughed, shaking their heads, almost in sync.

"How's about you two unhook all this 'n I'll go fix us some lunch?" Otis suggested, waving his hand from left to right.

"We ain't even had breakfast yet," Amos spoke up, laughing.

"Try beating the sun to rise," Otis returned as he went on his way toward the house.

"Beating the sun to rise?" I questioned Amos.

"He jus means waking earlier," Amos replied as we began to un-hook the chains.

"Where'd you come across this car?" I asked curiously.

"You too?" he questioned from under the car as I stood at his side.

"You ain't gotta say, I'm sorry, I was jus curious is all," I replied, kneeling down to see him.

"You had many jobs in your short time?" he asked as he banged around under the car.

"Not many, no," I replied.

"Well, as you do, you gonna run into different sorts 'uh people... two kinds really...the kind that pay...and the kind that don't," he explained as he slid out from under the car.

"Okay," I said simply as I nodded my head.

"I ain't dishonest, and I ain't no thief, but I also ain't about to let *anyone* take me for some fool," he went on as he pointed to the chains on the truck for me to unhook.

"I understand," I added as I knelt down to unhook the chains.

"Look, I worked and I worked and I worked, and there wasn't a single complaint that came outta me...*but then when it came time to pay what was owed to me, he refused, said I was lucky to have even been fed.* I saw the man put money in every other hand but mine, so

I made like I was walkin' off, and he laughed...but all that done was set me straight on gettin' what I was owed," he explained as he grabbed the chains from me and tossed them onto the deck of the truck.

"So those police that was chasin' you..." I started.

"That was on account 'uh him callin'," he interjected.

"What's gonna come 'uh this car now?" I asked as I stood to my feet.

"Don't know...see what *he* says I guess," he replied, pointing toward the house, speaking of Otis.

The two of us pushed the car back, closer to the shop, then Amos jumped in the truck and parked it next to the building. Just as he turned the engine off Otis called us to the house for lunch.

As the days were getting cooler the dew was late to lift and there was still a light fog lingering in the tall grass. Amos and I each grabbed some wood to carry into the house for fire.

"Sooo, you both welcome here, long as you need, but you gonna get that there car in order and back to where it came from...the both 'uh you," Otis ordered as we washed our hands to eat.

I looked up at Amos as he stood next to me, both of us scrubbing in the same basin, and he stretched a smile across his face, lifting his eyebrows.

"Understood?" Otis barked as he smacked his hand down the table.

"Yes sir," Amos and I replied in sync.

Amos winked at me, before turning to be seated at the table to eat. I smiled in return as I dried my hands and then sat down next him.

Eating together, the three of us, as we each gave a little bit more of ourselves to one another, was becoming quite pleasurable. The quality of care and attention was different than from being around women but still not without its own sense of warmth. I'd become used to gentle backrubs and little bits of affection wherever it could be shown, in any way, by being around Ms. Violet, and Mr. Charlie had his role of the more masculine-teacher-type, but in either relationship it was always coming from love, no question. Being here, with Amos and Otis, there was this back and forth that went on between us and we each had the room to say whatever we chose, respectfully, but I think deep down we all understood one another. Maybe that was from being abandoned, or left behind, or being brokenhearted, but we got it, and we sure laughed a lot.

After lunch, Amos and I cleaned up while Otis went outside to have a look at the car and assess the damage, or what he thought it was going to take to get it back in running condition.

"Think if you jus told him what happened, he won't make us take it back?" I questioned Amos.

"No, won't make much difference...and he's right anyway, it needs to go back," he replied.

"Thought you said..." I started.

"I was wrong in doin' what I did, and that's enough reason for it to go back," he explained as he handed me a plate to dry.

"But I thought..." I went on.

"Forget what you thought, and forget what I said, I was wrong, and I shouldn't be leadin' you to believe that it's okay to take what ain't yours, even if someone put you in a spot," he interrupted me to explain.

"I understand," I replied simply.

I understood where he was coming from in both manners. I could relate to him taking the car after being taken advantage of and him needing to not allow that to happen, but I could also relate to him knowing it wasn't right to do so. For as much as I wanted to relate *more* to him taking it, I appreciated his effort in guiding me toward the right decision.

Once we finished cleaning up we went outside.

"So?" Amos spoke up as we neared Otis, standing next to the car.

"It ain't so bad...at just a look. Might wanna make a fire in the shop stove and pull these seats out to give 'em the best shot at dryin' out evenly," Otis explained, puffing on his pipe.

"I can do that," I spoke up as I went to grab some wood from the pile.

The two of them circled the car together, looking at it, while Otis gave Amos instructions, but from what I could hear it was mostly just rambling. I laughed to myself as I thought of how Otis must have been enjoying himself, having something to do to break routine. Amos appeared to be just as happy to allow Otis to ramble, certain I'm sure, at how much he needed to do so.

I made my way into the shop, pulled the old canvas tarps off the windows to let more light in, and then began to make a fire.

Amos soon came in to see how I was making out, grabbed a few wrenches and then he went back outside.

Lucky was at my side with every move I made. The donkey started to act up out back and in between Otis shouting at it from beside the car, Lucky would let out a single bark, seemingly annoyed with the banter from both of them.

"He ain't gonna let up," Amos said as he came back into the shop.

"I'll try 'n keep him quiet," I suggested, looking down at Lucky.

"No...he ain't what I'm talkin' about," he replied, waving his arm.

He grabbed a piece of steel pipe and went back out toward the car; I followed, with Lucky right behind me.

Otis stood next to the car with both front doors open, hunched over, looking inside. As Amos approached the car Otis stood up straight and pointed to something within, while speaking softly to Amos. I went to the drivers' side to have a look at what was happening. Amos slid the piece of pipe over the wrench he had on a bolt for the seat, then he looked over at me and winked before he grunted with all of his might as he pulled on the pipe.

"Pull on that no good piece 'uh..." Otis shouted as he looked over at me, smiling.

I watched in anticipation just as Amos flew back against the inside of the open car door.

"She break?" Otis yelped.

"Think so," Amos replied as he propped himself up.

"You okay?" I asked of him.

"No sweat," he replied, smiling.

Amos slid the pipe off and began to loosen the bolt with just the wrench. With Otis continuing to hover as he gave his grandson direction on every last step, the process was repeated three more times, and soon enough the front seat was removed from the car.

We carried the seat into the shop and set it down just a few feet from the stove where I'd made the fire. I tossed in some more wood and we went back outside.

The banter continued back and forth between Otis and Amos while I enjoyed listening to it. Every so often one of them would turn to me and ask what I thought was so funny, but it seemed to be more of something to do just to break away from the moment. I laughed as much as I could get away with, while Lucky was at my side as we watched, and soon both Otis and Amos let up on each other and began to enjoy the day.

I'd never been around people who gave each other so much room to be themselves. Even when they were bickering it was all still okay; I enjoyed that, it felt right.

With the day gaining some heat and a light breeze upon the air, we left the doors open on the car and went to feed the animals out back.

Lucky went straight for the donkey, as did Otis, while Amos and I took some feed for the hogs and a bucket of grain for the hens.

Otis picked up his branch from the day before and began to smack the donkey, at its noisy request, while Lucky sat and watched in wonder.

"He always done that?" I questioned Amos.

"Would seem so. Can't figure though, how that animal managed to let him know to do such a thing, 'specially with him being tied up like that," he replied, curiously.

I squinted against the sun as I watched Otis lift the branch up above his head, then smack it down across the donkey's back, sides, and behind. In between serving his gentle lashings, he'd run his hand over its head and down its face then feed it a handful of grass as he spoke softly to it. Standing at the donkey's side, with a branch in one hand, wearing only boots and a wool blanket for a coat, while his large brimmed hat was pulled down so low it left little room to see his eyes, he was clearly *okay*. I smiled and laughed to myself at the sight of what most people would confuse as something being wrong in a man.

Amos carried on with feeding the animals as he talked to me while I watched Otis.

"Think that fire needs more wood?" I asked as I turned to Amos.

"Might," he replied simply, looking up at me.

"I'll go throw some on," I said as I gently patted one of the cows on its behind, in passing.

As I found myself in view of the shop I could see smoke billowing out the front doors. I looked back just once and then took off running into the building; I couldn't see anything. My lungs were rapidly filling with smoke as I tried to locate the source. With my hands stretched out in front of me, guiding my way by feel, I reached the handle on the stove door and quickly retracted as it was hot to the touch. I pulled my shirt off and wrapped it around my hand then grabbed onto the handle once more, lifted up on it, and swung the door open. With a cloud of smoke rushing to escape the small space of the stove, my lungs were quickly overwhelmed and I turned to find my way back out toward the light of the open shop doors. Gasping for air as I dropped to my knees, I began to cough as I looked around for Amos. My vision was blurring and I was having a hard time breathing in between coughing; all of which was quickly worsening. Everything went black.

I could hear the mumbling of voices around me but for some reason I couldn't open my eyes. I was reminded of my time in the creek when I was carried away by the current and there was a voice insisting that I *"stand up"*. I was searching for a similar sign or some guidance, only this time I couldn't place anything among the intrusive feelings and thoughts of uncertainty that were quickly taking up space.

CHAPTER 15

"Anything?" I heard a voice say as a door slammed shut.

"Nothing yet," another voice replied.

There was an odd odor filling the air, something I'd never smelled before; it was more of a stench than anything.

I heard the shuffling of heavy feet or boots and then a loud sneeze.

"Sure comin' down out there," the voice said, just as thunder rattled the building.

As I scanned my eyes across the backs of my eyelids a few times, hesitant to try and open them again for fear of not being able to, I received the nudge from a gentle voice saying, *"it's okay"*.

I inhaled deep through my nose then exhaled slowly out of my mouth as I opened my eyes.

"You're up, he's up!" the voice exclaimed.

It was Amos. I smiled as he stood over me, looking down with a smile of his own.

"Thank heavens, boy; you sure given us a good scare, you can bet!" Otis said in celebration as he smacked his hands together, appearing next to Amos.

I smiled as I shifted to sit up.

"No, no, not jus yet...you take a few minutes to gather yourself before you go movin' around," Otis insisted as he patted me softly on the chest.

"What happened?" I asked softly as I slowly laid back down.

"You was jus takin' a little stroll with God is all," Otis replied, smiling gently.

"The shop?" I questioned, concerned.

"She's still standing; it look like some birds got in there 'n made themselves a nest, pluggin' up the chimney," Amos spoke up.

"You shouldn't 'uh done what you did, but...thank you," Otis said softly.

I smiled in return to his words.

Thunder shook the house once again, followed by the even louder noise of Otis' donkey.

"You gonna be back out there in that weather quicker than a flash 'uh lightning if you can't get a hold 'uh yourself," Otis belted over his shoulder.

I sat up and looked over the back of the couch. There stood the donkey, just a few feet from me, tied up to the knob on the front door of the house. My jaw dropped open as I rubbed my eyes.

"He don't do well in storms," Otis explained in short.

"Lucky?" I asked of his whereabouts, not taking my eyes off of the donkey.

"Right outside, on the front porch," Otis replied, gesturing to the front of the house.

It was strange enough that there was donkey in the house, on account of its fear of storms, but then I couldn't make sense of how Lucky didn't manage to be invited inside.

"He was sure worried about you...bet he'd be happy to know you're okay," Amos said, encouragingly.

"I bet," I said softly, giggling.

"If he got his manners intact and ain't gonna stir up no trouble for *that one,*" Otis started, pointing at the donkey, "don't see why he can't come say hello," he finished as he went toward the front door.

"He won't, I'll even tell him so," I insisted as I was still staring at the donkey.

"Now you best behave yourself or you won't so much as be invited back past the property line...the two 'uh you figure yourselves out and let that be the end of it," Otis lectured Lucky as he stood at the front door, before letting him inside.

Otis propped open the screen door with his foot and then Lucky, lowering his head, scurried past the donkey and straight to my side, greeting me with great celebration.

Amos started to laugh as he began to pet Lucky, joining in the moment. Otis stood still at the door while he flip-flopped between scolding and speaking sweetly to the donkey, ensuring him of his departure had he chose to misbehave.

"If you so fond 'uh that animal, why ain't he got a name?" I asked of Otis as I parted from Lucky's attention for a moment.

"Figure it might jus be easier to lose him, if time sees it that way, without the burden of a name," he replied, leaving the donkey's side to go into the kitchen.

The storm was growing with intensity as the loud, crackling, and banging of thunder was quickly followed by streaks of lightning, one after the other, lighting up the dark sky.

Lucky found his way to the fireside as Otis and Amos prepared some food. The donkey remained as quiet as he could, aside from the clomping of his four, stubby, hoofed limbs smacking against the wood floor of Otis' entryway.

Soon, we were all seated at the table, eating.

"How long was I out for?" I asked curiously as there was break in conversation.

"Who can tell?" Otis replied casually as he filled his mouth with food.

"Sorry?" I looked over at Amos, confused.

Amos shrugged his shoulders and smiled.

"Two days...not long," Otis muttered without care in between bites.

"Two days?!" I blurted out in question.

"He's messin' with you...wasn't more than a few hours," Amos spoke up, gripping my hand with his.

I immediately turned my attention to Otis. He had his head down over his plate, and his shoulders were shaking as he tried to contain his laughter.

"You!" I belted.

He looked up at me, still laughing, and draped his large hand over my shoulder, then winked just once, nodding his head, and went back to eating.

I started to laugh and Amos soon joined in. Otis kept most of his laughter to himself, but nonetheless continued his short bursts in between bites of food as he stayed hunched over his plate.

With dinner finished and the dishes cleaned and put away, the three of us sat next to the fire and visited while the storm carried on with a seemingly great frustration, pouring down rain and rattling the house with each deep rumble of thunder.

Lucky cautiously whimpered as he looked toward the door. With just the screen door closed the fresh air being swept in was soon carrying on its back the stench of donkey dung. Otis stood to his feet to have a better look and sure enough, amidst the noise of the storm, the donkey managed to relieve himself on the floor of the house.

"You sorry son of a..." Otis scolded the ill-mannered animal as it stood in the doorway with a look of complete shame on its face.

Otis stepped outside onto the porch, grabbed a shovel, and then with a single swoop across the floor the mess was removed. He held a large rag outside under the falling of rain to soak it, and with a few trips back and forth, ringing it out and then soaking it again, the mess in its entirety was cleaned up. Otis managed all of this without breaking from his lecture and cursing through each breath; yet he didn't remove the donkey from the house.

"That ain't no lesson to become accustom to following 'round here neither," Otis said as he pointed at Lucky.

Lucky simply kept his head rested down on the floor beneath him and avoided eye contact with Otis. Amos ran his hand across Lucky's back a few times as we laughed.

"Why don't you spray some 'uh that pretty perfume you brought along?" Otis suggested as he sat back down.

"Sure thing," I replied, laughing, as I stood to get into my suitcase.

I stood at the doorway for a few moments, spraying it into the breeze that was still blowing in through the house. I then made a couple of rounds through the small living space as I continued to spray the warming scent of my grandmother, creating a very comforting tone among the air. I caught Otis slowly closing his eyes and taking in a few deep breaths through his nose, then smiling at its welcome arrival.

"Much better," Amos said of the change in scent upon the air.

Instead of putting the perfume back in my suitcase I left it on the table, next to the couch, in case of similar happenings in the near future.

Amos stepped outside to grab some more wood while I pulled out my harmonica and began slowly blowing into it as I sat back down.

"You play?" Otis questioned with delight.

"Not really," I replied in short, removing the harmonica from my lips to speak.

Otis got up and shuffled across the floor in his wool socks to the back room.

Me neither," he chirped as he came back holding an old guitar.

I smiled as he sat down across from me, perching the guitar upon his bare knee.

"Let's see what 'chu got," he insisted as he smiled, encouraging me.

I thought fondly of Mr. Charlie as I began to blow softly into the harmonica. Huffing and puffing as I did my best to catch a tune, Otis waved his hands to get my attention and he smiled as he politely asked me to stop.

"Try rollin' it back 'n forth in your hands or across your thigh for a minute...warm it up some," he suggested with care, still smiling.

I did as he said, while he messed with the strings on his guitar; strumming each one then adjusting it accordingly.

"Give it another go," he spoke, looking up at me.

Slightly hesitant, I softly blew into it again.

"C'mon now," he coaxed me. "Music, it's 'uh...it's a patient but courageous celebration...one that is simply awaiting your arrival," he explained with grace, smiling.

I closed my eyes and thought of the first time we'd had a fish fry, when Mr. Charlie and his friends were playing music bringing everyone, including myself, into dance.

I kept my eyes sealed tight as I continued to try and find a rhythm in my breathing while I slowly slid my way across the instrument, blowing softly, then inhaling the same, as I toyed with long and quick short bursts of air.

Otis began to clap lightly as he worked to build a beat for me and as soon as I caught up to his pattern he jumped in with his guitar.

With my eyes still closed I heard the footsteps of Amos approach the door and then enter the house. He didn't say anything as he quietly set the wood down and added some to the fire. The couch shifted next to me as his weight was added once he sat down; although I didn't skip a beat while Otis and I were still massaging the perfume-filled air with our attempt at music. Just as we seemed to find ourselves on the edge of harmony Amos bridged the gap with a voice that was surely intended for summoning the angels. I wanted to stop my efforts just to listen to him but I didn't want to chance him stopping as well, so I continued on, as Otis did the same.

I couldn't help but be reminded of my grandmother as the scent of her perfume still lingered, and the welcoming surprise of Amos' voice was so much like standing next to her in church; time simply stood still. As my exposure to music was quite thin I couldn't place the song he was singing, but it really didn't matter because it spoke directly to my soul.

I opened my eyes and slowly scanned the room to place each body, seeking the sources of what I was experiencing. Otis was still seated on the chair across from me with his eyes focused down on his guitar, and Amos, with his eyes closed, sat as still as the donkey stood, while he appeared to have found an escape for himself.

Amos brought his singing to an end as did Otis and I with our instruments.

"Amen!" Otis exclaimed as he strummed his last stroke.

I laughed with pure joy.

"You got somethin' in you," Amos said to me as he gently nudged his elbow into my side.

"Me?" I questioned as I leaned back in shock of his deflecting.

"Yes, you...you got somethin' special with that," he insisted, smiling.

"I wasn't doin' nothin' but blowin' hot air...you the one with *somethin' special*, like you said," I said joyfully.

"Your grandmother used to sing that to your mother when she was jus a little girl," Otis explained gently.

"And she would sing it to me, mom would...still 'bout the only song I know by heart," Amos said in return as he looked down at the floor.

With the storm persisting it would have been difficult to try and go to bed so we stayed up deep into the night, playing music, eating, and of course, laughing.

"So, jus how old are you anyway?" Otis asked of me as we sat by the fire.

"Don't quite know, jus had me my first birthday before my grand-mother died," I explained with ease.

"Your first?" he questioned curiously.

I simply nodded my head.

"Ain't that somethin'," he insisted, smiling with wonder.

"It is?" I asked.

"Sure it is; you could be a hundred and ten for all you know," he suggested, laughing.

"Can't see that," I replied slowly.

"Look, I ain't sayin' you is but, there surely ain't no downfall to *not* knowin' how old you are," he belted.

"There ain't?" I asked curiously.

"Nooo...nothin' good comes from time; not in years lived, not years dead 'n gone...there ain't nothin' curious about it, it's all containing, it keeps us in line, grieving, longing...it keeps us worried," he explained. "Life done you a favor in not knowin'...*you got magic in that,*" he added, smacking his hand against his knee.

Amos patted me on the back as he sat next to me.

Otis was right. I'd always had this sense of shame in not knowing my age because it was something that everyone around me had known of themselves, until I met Hope, and even then it still wore on me within; but Otis had just given me an entirely new way of not needing to depend on such a trivial piece of information.

The three of us, simultaneously, looked toward the front door at the sudden and loud noise coming from the donkey. He was sleeping, standing up, and began to snore like I'd never heard before; even Lucky raised his head in wonder. Otis stood to his feet, pulling the ratty wool blanket off the back of the chair he was sitting on and then went over to the donkey and draped it over its head, covering its eyes. With the steady hammering of thunder and its fear of storms, it was a wonder how he'd been able to fall asleep in such a manner.

Amos lightly dug his elbow into my side as we watched and worked to hear Otis speaking gently into the animals' blanket covered ear. He was so fond of that animal; it was really something else to watch.

Well into the night, and most likely quite early in the morning, Amos stoked the fire one last time and then we tucked ourselves into bed after Otis fed us a final snack before turning in himself.

Amos and I fought to find a volume to speak at with the donkey still snoring, until he fell asleep, and I shortly after.

CHAPTER 16

"Would you look at that!" Otis bellowed, waking me up.

It was daylight as he stood, staring out the front door.

"Whaaat?" Amos muttered into his pillow.

"What is it, what 'chu lookin' at?" I asked as I sat up, leaning back on my elbows.

"C'mon, come here, you gotta see this," Otis insisted, looking back at me.

I stood to my feet and slowly walked toward the front door where he stood.

My eyelids stretched open, certainly wider than ever before.

"Amos...get up, come look at this!" I chirped, waving my hand behind me, not taking my eyes off of it.

I stood still next to Otis as we were both quite obviously in the same state of awe.

The ground was completely white and the trees were covered the same, as well as everything in sight.

"What is it?" I asked of Otis in complete wonder.

"Snow...but it ain't never come this early before," Otis replied, sounding amazed.

"Snow?" I questioned curiously.

"Yeah, 'bout the only place it falls for a hundred miles in any direction. Can't say what brings it here, but it's always a nice surprise when it comes," he explained softly, staring out the screen door.

I'd never seen it before nor had I even heard of it, but it was absolutely beautiful.

"Amos!" I shouted with excitement.

"It ain't nothin' to him...he ain't too fond of it to begin with," Otis spoke up, looking back at Amos, still tucked under his blanket next to the smoldering fire.

"Think we can go outside?" I asked, still in awe.

"Get after it," he replied, smiling down at me.

"You comin'?" I questioned Otis.

"Right behind you...I best take this old mule out before he mistakes my floor for the dirt," he replied, pulling back the blanket from the animals' head.

I pushed open the screen door and tiptoed across the front porch in anticipation of my first introduction to snow.

"Ain't you gonna put no shoes on?" Otis belted from inside the house.

"Do I got to?" I asked, looking back.

"Nah, you ain't got to but, that snow's got a bite to it if you mess with it for too long," he answered as he guided the donkey outside.

I slowly made my way to the railing at the edge of the porch, which was covered in snow. I slid my hand into the fluffy, wet, white, wonderful but chilly surprise, as I closed my eyes. It was cold, quite quick, but worth every second as I smiled thinking of Hope, and even Ms. Violet, and how much they would surely love to see such a thing. Just as my heart began to ache, missing home, I received a smack in the face followed by the loud laugh of an old man in a wool blanket and boots standing next to a donkey who was now wearing socks.

At some point Otis had managed to dress the donkey in four mismatched socks, before leading him outside into the snow.

With how well the animal stood in those socks I'm certain it wasn't his first time being introduced to such an oddity. Funny to wonder though, how the two of them managed to conjure up such a thing.

Otis bent over, filled his hands with snow and then began to pack it, flipping it from one hand to the other. Before I could gather myself and realize what was happening, he cocked his arm back and threw the snow at me. Once again, it pelted me square in the face; I couldn't help but laugh.

"C'mon...gimme your best shot!" he shouted as he raised his arms in the air.

"How'd you do that?" I asked, laughing.

"You need me to come 'n throw it for you too?" he questioned playfully.

I scraped my hands across the railing, filling them with snow, and then began to pack it just as I had seen Otis do. Once it felt compact, I cocked back my arm and threw it with everything I had in me.

"Whoops, sorry!" I yelled as the donkey kicked up its hind legs after I struck it, missing Otis as the target.

The two of us continued to throw snowballs at each other as I worked my way down the stairs and into the snow. Lucky was nipping at my heels and then chasing each snowball as it took flight. It was, without question, one of the happiest and most enjoyed moments of my life.

Soon enough, Amos made his way outside and joined in on the fun. Otis and my laughing must have been what coaxed him out of bed. With each of us in a groove, throwing one snowball after the other, we managed to clear a significant area around ourselves of all the snow by the time we were done.

With my feet near numb to the touch I scurried back into the house and sat by the fire. I wanted to stay outside and play some more but Otis went to feed the animals and ordered me to go warm up.

Amos followed soon after and joined me by the fire, adding some more wood.

"I ain't never seen him play like that, not ever," Amos said, speaking of Otis.

"That was so much fun, I can't believe you don't like the snow," I said, laughing.

"It's never been like that for me...you done somethin' to him, he ain't never been so free before," Amos explained in a gentle tone.

"Maybe it ain't me, might jus be life is all," I replied, uncertain.

"Nah...it's you, he took to you in a way that made a change in him...I can see it," he continued.

I didn't know what to say. I thought about my grandmother and how she had appeared to change, right before she passed on, but that wasn't something I thought would be fair to share with Amos.

"Time does different things to people...maybe it's jus his time to be different," I rambled as I worked to think of something to say.

"You call it time, I call it you...whatever it is, it's nice to see," Amos explained as he stood up, adding a log to the fire.

"What we gonna do about that car?" I asked, rubbing my feet.

"We'll get it...and then we can get on our way," he replied, looking over his shoulder toward the front door.

I was excited to get home and see Hope, Ms. Violet and Mr. Charlie, to tell them all about my adventure and everything that I had seen, but just as I felt the excitement I became sad as I realized that all I had done was for me, and that I hadn't fulfilled my purpose of finding any miracles for Hope.

"What is it, what's wrong?" Amos asked of me as I became quiet.

I explained to him the concerns and fears that had just come to me.

"I really know nothing of miracles, but as I hear you talk about 'em it makes me wonder about my own life," he said, sounding saddened.

"Your feet thaw out?" Otis belted as he entered the house.

Neither I nor Amos said anything at first; we simply stared at the fire, remaining quiet.

"What's this all about?" Otis questioned as he sat down.

"I ain't so sure what I done here is right," I spoke softly.

"In what form?" Otis asked, leaning forward to hear me.

"I left the side of Hope, left home, everything, to try 'n find some miracles in the belief that I could do jus that, and I ain't even come close," I explained with a sense of shame.

"Come close?" Otis questioned, uncertain.

"Yes sir," I replied in short.

"You see much snow where you from?" he asked in a stern tone as he sat up straight.

"No, sir, first time was when you woke me...jus this mornin'," I answered, gripping one hand in the other.

"You feelin' sorry for yourself?" he questioned. "You know what I mean by that?" he asked sharply.

"Yes sir, I know what you mean," I replied, looking at Amos.

"Don't look at him, look at me...and enough 'uh this *sir* nonsense, I ain't some *man* lookin' to get my worth outta you, I'm your friend," he said calmly.

I slowly nodded my head, just once.

"What's this need you got to be sad, for you to find somethin' wrong?" he asked.

I just looked at him.

"By all accounts I'd say you ain't seen nothin' *but* miracles since you lef' home, you jus too busy *lookin'* to know any better," he continued, sitting back in his chair.

"How so?" I inquired.

"How so?" he started. "It don't snow for a hundred miles in any direction, and I ain't seen it here this early for as long as I been in these woods, and then it jus so happens to fall when you here, on the hunt for miracles as it were...you can't feel that, *in here*?" he finished, pointing to his chest.

I didn't respond.

"Do you know what a miracle does...what its purpose is?" he questioned as he leaned forward.

"No...guess I don't," I replied softly.

"A miracles' purpose is to give you hope...it's **hope.** So when your friend, Ms. Violet, was tellin' you to keep an eye out for miracles, she was sayin' to **keep hope**. Hope is the birthplace 'uh faith...and by way 'uh faith, *everything* is possible. A miracle ain't no good to you if, well, it can't even appear if you ain't open to it. The only place a miracle can touch is your soul, your spirit, your heart...and if you too busy lookin' up, tryin' to bag a shooting star, *you gonna miss the snow right there at 'chur feet*. I can't say what's gonna come 'uh your friend or what a miracle will or won't do, that ain't for me to speak on, but I will say this...your little body is carrying a heart that would seem is too big, *I'm sure*, for even the largest of men, and I can only imagine that you been through a lot for a boy of your years, but everything in this world is gonna be drawn to you, 'cause 'uh your heart, 'cause 'uh your goodness, and your will...so you need to stop lookin' for miracles, they ain't out there to be seen, they in here, to be felt; feel it, feel everything in every moment you given, as you are...and hope will do the rest, *hope will lead you to faith*; and from faith, well..." he explained, patting his hand over his heart.

Just as I looked over, Amos was wiping a tear from his cheek as he'd had his back to Otis, listening to every word.

"She prob'ly already up 'n wanderin' around lookin' for you," Amos started, laughing. "Even you was out cold from that smoke 'n it ain't stop you from comin' to," he added, looking back at Otis.

I laughed as I looked at Otis, who had also begun laughing. As we all shared in a long, loud, bout of laughter, I felt a sense of ease come over me as I thought of everything that Otis had just shared with me and how I was probably just in a state of worry because of how sudden my grandmother had passed. I thought of how Prophet had spoken with similar words to me in the woods and how even Ms. Violet and Mr. Charlie didn't seem all that concerned with the condition of Hope; and then I remembered them promising to take her to the doctor if nothing came to change. I let out a big sigh of relief as I finished laughing.

Otis got up and began to prepare some food. I went into the kitchen to help where I could; he smiled and involved me as he saw fit, while Amos set the table.

After we ate the three of us went outside to do some chores and check on the animals. Otis shared his concerns of not having enough bedding for the animals as he thought we might get another storm and snowfall, so he started up the truck and we were preparing to go out in search of some. Amos hoisted Lucky up onto the flat deck and then the three of us packed ourselves into the cab to head out.

"Ohhh, well you sure smell pretty," Otis teased me, speaking of my grandmothers' perfume.

"Don't he?" Amos blurted out as he laughed, nudging me in the ribs.

I looked over at Otis as he smiled, then Amos the same, and I simply smiled in return knowing full well that they both enjoyed the scent, no matter how much they teased me.

The trail was a lot rougher heading out than it was just days before when we retrieved the car from the lake, so Otis was travelling at an even slower speed. I kept looking out the back window to check on Lucky; he appeared to be enjoying himself as he was walking laps around the edge of the deck.

"He ain't goin' nowhere," Otis shouted over the loud noise of the engine.

I smiled and nodded.

As we neared the lake Amos elbowed me and pointed to where we had leapt from the car, leaving it to roll into the water. Bouncing back and forth in my position between him and Otis I laughed, as did he, at the not so distant memory.

Otis shook his head as he shifted gears, smacking the shifter against my leg, pinning me tight to the seat, and just as he'd done before, he lightly tapped my leg and apologized. Once we were out on the road he began to pick up speed, freeing my legs of the abuse.

It was true; there was no snow to be seen once we were out of the forest and on our way down the road. The snow was quickly blowing off the truck as Otis gained speed, leading me to be all the more amazed, as though we had just left an entirely different world. I leaned forward, holding on to the small dash of the truck as I peered out the window in awe of the change. It was sunny, there was dust swarming upon the surface of the road and there wasn't a cloud in the sky. The further we went, the more I relaxed and soon sat back in my spot.

With time passing and the noise of the engine being so loud that none of us bothered to try and speak over it, Amos began to get restless. He kept pulling on my ear and then he'd smack my thigh when I went to cover my ear. This went on for a few minutes until I squirmed so much that I'd knocked the transmission out of gear, hitting the shifter with my leg, and with Otis still having his foot down on the gas pedal the engine started to howl.

"You fools, you gonna leave us stranded...keep messin' around 'n see!" Otis barked as he fought to find a gear.

"Yeah, Poor Boy, see what 'chu done!" Amos chimed in, laughing.

"You was pickin' at him," Otis spoke up as he managed to get the truck back in gear.

I didn't speak, I just looked at Amos and laughed, keeping my face out of view from Otis.

"You two...better than any brothers, I'm sure," Otis said as he smacked me on the thigh, seeming to have calmed down.

It wasn't long before we were slowing down and making a turn into a farmyard.

"We here?" I questioned Otis.

"We here," he replied, pulling up to the house as he unrolled his window.

"You'll find him in the shop!" a woman shouted as she stepped outside to greet us, pointing toward a row of buildings.

"Figured as much...jus thought I'd stop in, thank you," Otis replied, just as he'd shut the engine off.

The woman waved a white towel, which she had draped over her shoulder, and then closed the door.

Otis started the engine and we slowly made our way across the yard to the shop, which the lady at the house was speaking of.

"Wait here, I'll be back," Otis said as he stepped outside the truck.

I looked back to check on Lucky.

"He look thirsty," Amos said as he opened the door to get out.

"But he said to wait," I said in return.

"Ain't no harm in gettin' your dog somethin' to quench his thirst," he replied as his feet hit the ground.

"Yeah, guess you right," I said as I followed him.

"C'mon, let's have a look around," he insisted as I began to pet Lucky, who was standing at the edge of the deck.

"You sure we should?" I asked of him.

"What...you scared?" he teased me.

"Nah...I ain't scared 'uh nothin'," I replied as I stepped forward to follow his lead.

We walked toward the first building, leaving Lucky on the truck. Amos opened the door and went in; I followed. It was dark and smelt of rotten feed. Leaving little to the imagination, we turned back, closing the door behind us. Approaching the next building, Amos pulled his shirt up over his nose and went inside. I waited outside the door.

"Get in here," he instructed, softening his voice.

I covered my nose with my hand and slowly walked inside. The sun was shining in through a large hole in the roof, blinding me for a moment, as I quickly raised my hand to shield my eyes. Before I could adjust my sight, there was a large-winged bird coming straight at me. I screamed like an infant, turning to run outside as I tripped on the ledge, landing facedown with half my body still in the building. I rolled over onto my back as I heard the loud roar of Amos' laughter. He stood over me, taunting, holding a bird in his hands as he flapped the wings. I scurried backwards on my back-side, using my hands and feet to carry me across the ground.

"Relax...it ain't even got a heartbeat," he belted as he continued to laugh, flapping its wings.

I stood to my feet, brushing off my legs and arms, scowling at Amos.

"Thought you wasn't scared 'uh nothin'?" he teased, still laughing.

I didn't respond; I stood still, squinting against the sun as I worked to calm my quick beating heart.

"Boys!" Otis shouted as he appeared from inside the shop.

"We was jus lookin' to get Lucky some water," Amos and I said simultaneously as we turned to see Otis.

"There's a rain barrel at the side of the shop," a man said as he stepped outside, pointing to the side of the building.

"Boys...this here's Mr. Day...we go back a long ways," Otis explained in short as he looked to his friend.

The man stood at the side of the truck, petting Lucky, with a cigar hanging from his mouth. He was wearing glasses and had dark wavy hair and a moustache, with hints of grey in both. I caught the faint sounds of him wheezing as he stood stroking Lucky, wearing overalls, no shirt, and some tattered boots. He had a very warm quality about him as we all engaged in a brief visit. He was hanging on to every word that was uttered, awaiting the perfect moment where he would then jump in with something quick witted, sending us all into laughter.

"Well...best get that water so we can move on," Otis instructed us.

"Should be a saucer on the floor next to the press," Mr. Day said as he pointed to the shop.

I grabbed the saucer and filled it with water then slowly walked with it back to the truck to give to Lucky. Mr. Day took it from my hands, winking at me, then set it down and slid it in front of Lucky.

Lucky had the water cleaned up and the saucer empty in no time; then Otis and Mr. Day jumped into the cab while Amos and I climbed onto the deck with Lucky, before setting out across the yard and into the field.

Otis pulled up next to a large stack of straw bales and then shouted at us from the cab to load up a dozen. Amos leaped off the deck and climbed onto the top of the stack then began tossing bales, one by one, onto the truck for me to pile. Lucky got in between the bales and the back of the cab, appeared to be content, and stayed there. It wasn't long before we finished and were heading back toward the shop.

After a short visit in the yard we said our goodbyes, got back in the truck, and drove off; but not without Mr. Day sending us on our way with one of his wife's freshly baked pies, and a few more of his jokes.

The ride back was much of the same; Amos poking and prodding at me while Otis worked to ignore it, until we managed to get too rowdy and then he'd slow down and threaten us with having to walk the rest of the way. He never stayed angry for long though and quite often he just seemed annoyed because he couldn't join in.

We weren't halfway through the forest before it started to snow so heavily that you couldn't see ten feet in front of the truck. I gripped on to the dash in complete awe as Amos had his head out the window, verbally working to guide Otis upon the trail as we slowly crawled along.

"Dammit!" Otis cursed out as we hit something, forcing the truck to stall out.

"What is it?" I questioned curiously, still blinded by a thick white blanket of snow.

"Best jump out 'n have a look," he replied as he swung open his door to step outside.

Otis' feet didn't touch the ground before Amos and I were both outside at the front of the truck. With the three of us kneeling down to have a look underneath the truck, it quickly became apparent why we had stopped so suddenly.

"You managed to catch that stump back there, but this you couldn't see?" Otis mocked Amos, speaking of the large boulder which the truck now sat upon.

"You was supposed to be lookin' too," Amos shouted at him. *"How was I gonna see that when it's so far over?"* he finished, waving his hand in the air as we all stood to our feet.

"How far are we from the house?" I asked Otis.

"Tough to say," he replied with a grunt.

"Think you can work your way down off that?" Amos questioned Otis.

"Can't hurt to try," he shouted as he went toward the drivers' side door.

The wind was blowing in these bursts where it would calm for a minute and then pick up for several, making it hard to see or hear as we spoke to each other.

Amos grabbed me by the arm as I shouted for Lucky, pulling me back out of the way. Just as Otis began to rev the engine and drop it into gear, Lucky found his way to my side, barking with a great annoyance.

The frame of the truck sat quite high as it was, but now with it being hung up on a big boulder, the front tire was near a foot off the ground. I didn't say anything but I just couldn't see how he was going to wiggle his way off of it.

We watched countless attempts of Otis revving the engine and then slamming it into gear as we could hear it grind in his doing so, while he worked the steering to try and maneuver his way off of the rock. No such luck. Not before long, he shut the engine off and hopped out.

"Looks like we hoofin' it," Otis spoke out, pulling his hat down as we approached.

"Guess so," Amos replied, squinting against the blowing snow.

"You gonna be okay like that?" Otis questioned me on how I was dressed.

"Don't got much choice," I belted.

"You want my jacket?" Otis asked me.

"No thank you, you keep it...might need it more than I do," I replied as the three of us were huddled together.

I was weary of what he had on, and if in fact he had anything underneath that old wool blanket he wore so fondly.

The air was oddly warm but the snow and wind, when it would gust, was quite cold; it was something else.

With Lucky taking the lead, we set out for the house.

"What about the bedding?" I questioned Otis as we made our way.

"We gonna get it," he insisted.

The snow seemed to get thicker as it blew, the further we got from the truck. Lucky kept a close distance ahead of us and would bark every thirty seconds or so just to keep us in line with him; it was neat to see him take the lead so instinctively like that. We went on for what seemed like forever, until Lucky's bark gained in distance.

With the open clearing of Otis' small spread of land, there was no mistake once we neared the house. As Lucky let out a few quick barks, the donkey then followed suit from behind the house with his incessant racket; both, I'm sure, just as joyous in their own right with our return.

Otis directed us to the house to warm up and get a change of clothes. Amos and I carried in some wood and built a fire while Otis fixed us a quick bite to eat. After we ate and had managed to get our body temperatures back to near normal, Otis handed me an old one piece, cotton lined pair of overalls, and Amos was given a thick wool coat. The pant legs and arms were far too long on the overalls for me so, with the help of Amos, we rolled them up and he ran a loose stitch through each limb to keep them in place. Otis, still bare legged in just boots and his blanket, stood by the door waiting on us as he stared outside running dialogue with the weather. Once we were all ready we set out across the yard.

"You boys wanna grab the sleigh and I'll go get *what's his name*," Otis suggested as he pointed to the back of the house.

"Will do," Amos replied simply.

"What's his name?" I asked of Amos.

"He's talkin' 'bout that mule," he replied, rolling his eyes.

I shook my head, laughing, as I followed Amos' lead behind one of the smaller buildings.

"Think it's back here," he spoke out.

We came upon the sleigh; with grass wrapped tightly around its weathered, jagged skis, we worked to free it from the ground which it had settled into. Amos rocked it from side to side as I kicked at the ground to clear away the binds which the long grass had worked so well to create. Just as Otis came around the corner with a smart remark and the donkey, we had it free.

"Good show!" Otis belted as he raised his hands in the air, which jolted the donkeys' head upward.

Amos and I shifted the lead on the sleigh so Otis could get in with the donkey and hook him up; which he did in no time at all.

"You good...boys, ready?" Otis questioned us.

"Ready," I replied as Amos nodded his head.

Otis gave the donkey a light smack on its backside and off we went.

Lucky joined us as we crossed though the yard, and seemingly envious of the donkeys' role he got out in front and worked to keep it that way as he'd look back and bark every so often, almost mocking his less familiar companion.

Amos lightly hopped onto the edge of the sleigh then pulled me up to join him, while Otis stayed out front next to the donkey talking to it and stroking its back, keeping a slow but steady pace in an effort to not tire him out.

"Cut it out, you're gonna strain him," Otis shouted as Amos was trying to wrestle with me on the sleigh.

"He's a big boy, he'll be fine," Amos replied, laughing, as he ran his hand across my head.

"I ain't talkin' 'bout him...you're messin' around is jarring this poor animals' neck," Otis said in return.

I laughed and quietly mocked Amos for once again catching heck from his grandfather. It was funny to watch and then be able to tease him for it; I'd never experienced such a thing before. Otis enjoyed it just the same; I think it encouraged him to have a purpose, even if just for those brief moments, he was able to be a part of something. And Amos, well, he didn't bat an eye at any of it; he was just like a big kid.

By the time we neared the truck it was almost dark in the woods, so Amos lit the lanterns we'd brought, hung one on the front of the sleigh, and walked in front of the donkey and Otis with the other to help turn him around before we loaded the bales.

"Easy you stubborn mule..." Otis bellowed at the animal.

Lucky chimed in, barking. Otis and Amos led the donkey behind the truck to turn around but it was going too wide and ended up dragging the sleigh onto the side of an embankment at the back of the truck, nearly tipping it on its side.

Otis ran over to steady the donkey and keep it from moving any further while Amos pushed up against the sleigh and I worked to unhook the animal as fast as I could, with the instruction from Otis. As soon as I unhooked it from the sleigh Otis led him alongside the truck and out of the way. Amos and I dragged the sleigh back on level ground to a spot where we could load up the bales and be gone with ease.

As Amos tossed the bales off the truck, I stacked them on the sleigh while Otis held on to the donkeys' rope with one hand and held a lantern in the other. The wind was beginning to pick up and the blowing snow was becoming thicker.

"Of all the times not to cover your legs," Amos teased Otis as we worked to finish loading up in the blowing snow.

"Don't bother me none," Otis replied, lifting up the lantern.

"How many we takin'?" I asked Otis.

"Jus half for now...he won't handle much more," he answered simply.

Just as we got the last of the bales on, Otis hooked up the donkey to the sleigh once more. With the weight being significantly more on the way back, Amos and I were stuck to walking as well.

For all that the day had offered, in all of its adventure, walking back to the house next to a donkey pulling a sleigh across the snow covered ground as it continued to blow relentlessly, in a forest where only *it* was exposed to that weather, with two men I'd only known for a few days, in the dark lit by lanterns, with my dog leading the way...I was truly happy.

When we got back to the yard we threw the bales off and laid them out for the animals; some in the pigpen, some in the chicken-coop, and the rest for the cows. And of course, the donkey followed us into the house and was tied up to the door, where he would sleep once again. Otis said it was because we didn't have enough bedding for him, but Amos and I knew otherwise as we teased Otis.

We ate a late meal, all of us pitching in, and then Otis and I played some music while Amos smacked his knees and the donkey clomped his sock covered hoofs where he stood, before each of us washed up and went to bed at the fireside.

CHAPTER 17

After breakfast the next morning, we loaded up a jack and some tools onto the sleigh and we set out to retrieve the truck and the rest of the bales. The snow was still coming down but not as heavy as the night before so we were all a lot lighter in our step.

When we got to the truck Amos and I offloaded the last of the bales onto the sleigh while Otis worked to find a vantage point to jack the truck up. Once the truck was raised high enough off the boulder it sat on, Amos and I collected some deadfall and stacked it under the frame so that the jack could be removed.

"Get outta there!" Otis shouted as he jumped back.

Just as he'd pulled the jack out the truck rolled back; and neither I nor Amos were close enough to be harmed, I think it was just the natural reaction for Otis to shout like he did.

"Well that wasn't how I pictured it happenin' but, that'll do," Otis spoke out as he walked around to the passenger side.

The truck had managed to roll right off the boulder, leaving it free and clear to get in and drive away.

"Good enough!" Amos belted as he smacked me on the back, forcing me forward in my step.

Otis went ahead with the donkey and sleigh while Amos and I were going to take the truck, following behind.

"You gettin' anxious to get back home?" Amos asked me as we sat, waiting for the truck to warm up.

"I was..." I replied, looking over at him.

"But now you ain't?" he asked.

"I jus...I ain't never lived like this before. I do miss home...I miss Hope, Ms. Violet, and Mr. Charlie, but..." I worked to explain myself.

"But what?" he followed up, leaning over the steering wheel.

"I jus ain't never lived like this before," I repeated, watching my breath as it filled the cab in the cool air.

"It's different...how we been spendin' time?" he inquired gently.

"Different?" I started. "Could say that, yeah...but it don't really mean nothin' usin' such a word," I stated as I smiled.

I never put much thought into how my life would turn out, even when Hope and I were daydreaming and sharing with each other the things we wished upon, my future always looked a lot like the past, which I'd known so well. And then from the moment I saw Amos speeding by me in that car as he was being chased by the police, life just began to reveal itself to me; even more so as I worked to remain open.

"You like sugar?" he asked, smiling, as he reached into his pocket.

"You know someone that don't?" I returned, teasing.

"Found these when I put it on...he musta' been feedin' them to that mule," he said as he opened his hand to reveal some sugar cubes.

I laughed as I picked one from his hand and slowly set it on my tongue. I closed my eyes as I thought of Hope and our last moments together when we ate an entire jar full before going out into the forest; before she collapsed.

"What-chu laughin' at?" he asked as he put the truck into gear.

I told him what I was thinking about; he smiled and then smacked me on the leg.

"You know, it's possible to have too much sugar like that all at once...maybe that's what had her sick. This guy I was workin' with, on that farm, had the same thing happen from sugar, and he was better in a day or two," he explained with encouragement as we slowly crawled along.

"That true?" I questioned curiously.

"True as the sun, he passed out, right there in front of us...and that was a grown man," he replied, wiping the inside of the windshield with his sleeve.

"And he got better?" I asked, eager to know.

"Like new," he insisted, smiling.

I smiled as I rubbed my hands across the tops of my legs, suddenly filled with hope and a greater sense of certainty.

"You young yet, and you ain't seen a whole lot away from home, so it's natural to worry...but don't, there ain't no need for it," he explained with care.

"I understand," I humbly replied.

"Tell yah what...we'll make a point to gettin' that car done, and then you 'n me will take a ride 'n you can see for yourself...beyond that, you can decide what you wanna do," he suggested with enthusiasm.

"Okay," I returned, smiling.

"Prob'ly best anyway, sounds like them folks care a great deal about you," he stated.

As quick as I was to think about never wanting to go back, I was suddenly excited to do just that.

"Look at that...you ever seen a man speak so common to an animal?" he blurted out as we approached Otis.

We laughed, watching as Otis was walking next to the donkey while it pulled the sleigh, nearing the yard. He was quite animated, holding on to a branch, as he'd look over at the donkey and then raise his hands in the air, clearly telling it some type of story or anecdote. Lucky trailed behind the sleigh as he looked back at us, approaching, seemingly in despair from the banter in which Otis was feeding his beloved donkey; as though he'd purposely lagged behind to avoid it.

"He sure somethin' else," I replied as I had scooted forward on the seat to have a better look.

Otis looked back, raised his stick in the air, and then motioned for us to pass as we crawled into the yard.

Amos parked the truck then we walked over to meet Otis, offload the bales and spread them out for the animals, while he then un-hooked his stubby friend from the sleigh.

"I ain't never seen no sleigh like that before," I said to Amos as we tossed around the bales.

"He built that...had wheels on it at one point but they didn't sit well when it wasn't bein' used, so he made up them skis 'n never had another problem...'specially in this snow," he explained.

"He really different now...like you say he was?" I asked as I ducked into the low standing shelter to spread out some straw.

"Sure is...he ain't even like the first day we was here. You brought somethin' out in him, jus you bein' you, even a fool would see that... he's lighter," he replied as he threw another bale over the fence, into the pen.

"Me bein' me?" I questioned curiously.

"You...yes, you...you ain't like most people, Poor Boy, and you sure ain't nothin' like anyone he been around when he chooses to venture out," he said without thought.

"I ain't?" I asked as I stood still.

"No, you ain't...and that ain't near a bad thing, so don't concern yourself with it," he demanded as he stopped working to say so.

"Got 'er?" Otis bellowed as he neared the fence.

"Almost," I spoke up.

Otis stood, leaning on the fence, as he watched us finish spread out the bedding for the animals.

Amos asked if we needed to put some out for the donkey but Otis was quick to decline as he reasoned with how hard the animal had worked over the past twelve or so hours. I just laughed, as I'd come to do when he spoke about almost anything, but in particular that donkey.

"Ahh, he can sit outside 'till nightfall...see how the weather turns," Otis grumbled with no certain direction.

"You suppose it's gonna be like this for long?" I asked.

"Can't say for sure...it comes and goes like this 'till spring," he explained, looking up to the sky.

We finished up with the chores then Amos and I went to go see about the car while Otis wandered around, completing some odds and ends to welcome the snow, before going into the house to fix supper.

The car seats had managed to dry out so we took to the tools and bolted them back in; but not before we made sure the chimney in the shop was clear of any obstructions and we lit a fire.

Once the seats were back in Amos tried starting the engine; no luck. We messed around with everything he could think of but it just wouldn't fire. It wasn't long before he sent me to go get Otis for some help.

Otis had his hands under the hood for no longer then it would take me to gut a fish and he had the car started.

I wanted to know what it was that he did but there was a bigger part of me that wanted to let him keep it to himself, as I could see him shine on behalf of his knowhow.

I poured the last of the fuel from one of Otis' gas cans into the car as it ran for a few minutes while the two of them tinkered under the hood.

Amos had me shut the engine off and the three of us stood around the shop visiting for a short while before going into the house for supper.

With it being our last meal together, Otis insisted on celebrating. He lit candles, he drank a single glass of homemade wine, and he even gave me a taste; it was disgusting. We laughed, as we'd come to do at meals or just by being in each others' company, sharing in stories or simply listening to Otis tell his.

As the food cleared, finding its way into our bellies, Otis stood to his feet and went to the stove. He had his back to us as he fidgeted at the counter and then he turned and began to sing. Amos turned to see Otis and he too joined in. As Otis made his way, just a few feet back to the table, he carried the pie which Mr. Day's wife had given to us, and standing in it was a single lit candle.

"Happy birthday dear Poor Boy...happy birthday to you!" they finished in sync, both smiling from ear to ear as Amos began to clap.

"What's this?" I asked, laughing.

"Can't hurt to have a second birthday, can it?" Otis questioned with a big smile as he set the pie down in front of me.

"Make a wish!" Amos insisted with cheer, smacking his hand down on the table.

"A wish?" I asked curiously.

"Yeah, and then blow it out," Amos replied, pointing at the candle.

"Close your eyes, make yourself a wish, and then blow out the candle," Otis instructed softly, standing over me.

I did just as they said, then as Otis grabbed the candle out of the pie and set it down next to my plate, tears began to roll down my cheeks; I was overwhelmed. Neither of them brought any attention to it, Amos simply set his hand on my shoulder for a moment while Otis slid a piece of pie in front of me and then brushed his hand across the top of my head.

Otis served Amos a piece of pie, then one for himself, and we all took a brief moment before looking at each other and then slowly beginning to pick away at the sweet treat set before us.

"Everything in life is simple: a tree, its leaves, a rose, you, me, us...yet it is all a contradiction because it is full of magic, full of wonder, it is miraculous. A simple boy from a simple but maybe unfair life, has brought magic into mine, has brought a miracle into my life. Joy will always wait, *patiently,* it waits for the dance to be celebrated...and you my young friend, have stirred something in me," Otis explained eloquently as he leaned on the table.

I looked over at Amos, who was smiling.

"Loss will do different things to a man, and it becomes easy to hide in, even into the depths of the woods you can try to escape...but you can only hide for so long before the message finds you," Otis continued, smiling at me.

"The message?" I asked quietly.

"Hope," he insisted softly, raising his eyebrows.

"And where there's hope, faith is born?" I questioned him.

Exactly! he exclaimed, smacking his hand down on the table.

"And what is faith?" I asked curiously.

He took a moment as he looked around, as if trying to find the words.

"You know when you go to sleep at night, 'n you lyin' there, thinkin' 'bout tomorrow, maybe even seven days from now, planning your day 'n what not?" he suggested.

"Yes," I replied simply.

"That!" he belted with enthusiasm.

"I'm sorry?" I asked, uncertain.

*"You just **believe** that you gonna wake up,"* he explained in a very comforting tone.

Amos began to laugh in a very sincere and almost euphoric way, as if it spoke directly to him; and I couldn't help but to join in, with Otis following immediately after.

The three of us sat and visited at the table for a while before we cleaned up, together, and then we sat around the fireplace, playing some music.

Otis insisted that I take a bath as I would be going home the following day and should look and smell as though I'd been taking care of myself; he boiled some water for me and that's just what I did.

Amos came to the bath side and had a look at my stitches, which he said weren't quite ready to come out, so he gently scrubbed it and ran some clean water over the wound. He said that we should leave it without a bandage overnight so it could get some air, but he instructed me not to sleep on it and then he'd check it again in the morning before we left.

"Gonna miss you around here," he suggested softly.

"I'm gonna miss you too," I replied, looking up at him.

I'd never said goodbye to anyone before, not with them still being alive.

"I ain't never been easy on you...never treated you like you deserved, but, if you didn't have the kindness that you do, surely from your mother herself, this young man never would've ended up here," Otis spoke to Amos as he joined us while I finished up bathing.

"That's okay, grandpa...it's okay," Amos replied, smiling.

"It's not, Amos, but thank you, you're a good boy," Otis insisted as he gripped onto the shoulder of Amos.

Amos nodded his head, smiling, as he turned to hug Otis; they embraced each other for a few minutes as I stood to dry myself off.

Once we were all washed up and visited for short while longer, we said our goodnights and went to bed. Amos and I stayed awake, talking, at the mercy of the donkeys' snoring, until he too fell asleep. I was feeling anxious to get home and sad about leaving so I remained awake, staring at the fire.

I got up and went into my suitcase.

"Otis, you up?" I whispered as I stood at his bedroom doorway.

"What's wrong?" he asked from the darkness of his room.

"Jus wanted to give you somethin'," I said quietly.

"Come, come, what is it?" he returned as he sat up.

"Jus a few things I had with me...might be more use to you than me," I explained as I handed him my grandfathers' coat and hat.

He began to laugh.

"Thank you, Poor Boy, thank you," he insisted with pleasure as he gripped them in his big hands.

"No thanks needed...I think you stirred somethin' in me also," I replied, smiling, as I turned to leave the room.

"Goodnight, son," he replied quietly.

"Goodnight," I whispered.

CHAPTER 18

The next morning while we ate breakfast I asked Otis if he had anything that I could use to put some snow in to bring home. He said he'd search something out once we were done eating and ready to go.

After we tidied up Otis went in search of a container while Amos and I waited for his return.

"I want you to have this," I said to Amos as I handed him the small piece of my grandmothers' mirror, which I'd pulled out from my suitcase.

He took it from my hand, looking at me with uncertainty.

"I jus think you need to see how beautiful you are when you be singin'," I suggested with a smile as I kneeled down on the floor in front of him.

He smiled as he looked down into the mirror.

"You somethin' else, Poor Boy...I sure am gonna miss you," he replied with a compassionate chuckle.

"You boys ready?" Otis belted as he entered the house.

"Ready," Amos and I replied in sync, looking at each other.

"Good, let's go," Otis demanded as he went into his bedroom.

"Let's?" Amos asked, shrugging his shoulders.

"You didn't think I was gonna let you go alone...be the only one to know where our young friend lay his head...did you?" Otis replied from his bedroom.

"Well, I jus..." Amos started.

"Jus what...suppose I wanna go for a visit, I gotta wait for you?" Otis prodded playfully.

I laughed joyously.

"So, how do I look?" Otis asked as he came out from his room.

"Like you know what you doin'," I replied, smiling.

He came out of his bedroom wearing the jacket and hat that I'd given to him; he'd also put on a pair of pants.

The three of us, with Lucky trailing behind, went outside to the car. I stood, with my hand on the door handle, looking around, taking it all in one last time as the scent of my grandmothers' perfume, catching the breeze, filled my nose.

"Go on, you ride up front," Otis insisted as he nudged me out of the way so he could get in the backseat.

"Why's the trunk lid up?" Amos asked as he went to the back of the car.

"The boy wanted snow!" Otis shouted from the backseat.

I got out to look; there was an empty oil drum filled with snow, standing upright in the trunk of the car.

"Think you got enough?" Amos teased him as he and I began to laugh.

"Well..." Otis started.

"See how much 'uh that we can keep," Amos suggested as we sat inside the car, looking back at Otis who was smiling, seated next to Lucky.

Off we went, in a stolen car that smelt like burning logs and had a trunk filled with snow.

After we managed to slowly make our way through the snow and out of the woods, we came onto the road under a perfect overcast which was certain to extend the lifespan of the gift I had hopes of delivering before it melted.

Otis played around in the backseat with Lucky, working to annoy Amos, I'm sure, as payback for us doing the same to him when he was driving; although Amos wasn't easily bothered so it just became amusing for us to watch and listen to.

Once we neared the diner where Amos and I had first met, I soon became familiar with my surroundings and was able to give the proper directions.

The closer we got to home the more anxious I became and soon found myself fidgeting and unable to sit still.

"Relax...it's okay," Amos said as he looked over at me.

Once we drove by the church it hit me on how long I'd been gone. Even for as short as it was I'd never been away before, so seeing familiar buildings brought on an odd sense of new life; I was seeing things differently.

As we pulled into the yard I directed Amos to park behind my grandmothers' house. Getting out of the car I looked around in hopes of seeing a familiar face but there was no one in sight.

Otis and Amos soon stepped out and I showed them into the house, but surely not before Lucky entered; he who felt the need to barge his way through.

The house was clean and the note which I left behind was still sitting on the table. I gave Amos and Otis the grand tour of my grandmothers' small house and then put some water on to boil for tea, as they didn't want to leave before they knew I was okay; even after I'd insisted that I was.

The three of us sat visiting at the kitchen table, but mostly just avoiding discussing the whereabouts of the people who I so affectionately had been speaking of.

"Baby...that you?" a familiar voice spoke out.

It was Ms. Violet. I quickly stood up and ran outside to greet her.

I ran straight into her open arms and didn't let go.

"Where was you all this time?" she asked as she squeezed me in her grip. "We was worried sick," she stated.

I grabbed her by the hand and led her into the house.

"Otis, Amos...I'd like you to meet, Ms. Violet," I said as Amos and Otis quickly stood to their feet.

"It's a real pleasure to meet you, ma'am...this young one has a great deal 'uh kind things to say about you," Otis said as he extended his arm to shake her hand.

Ms. Violet smiled as she embraced his gesture.

"Nice to finally meet you, Ms. Violet," Amos insisted with a smile as he too, gently shook her hand.

"Baby, where you been?" she asked of me in a soft tone.

"I got so much to tell you, ma'am, I can't even think 'uh where to start...come outside, I wanna show you somethin', you won't believe this," I rambled as I grabbed her by the hand to go outside.

Amos and Otis followed eagerly, with Lucky lagging behind.

*"Now, where's Hope, we need Hope, where Mr. Charlie at?...They gonna wanna see this, I know they ain't **never** seen nothin' like it!"* I insisted, excited, looking around.

"Jus slow down a moment, child, slow down," she replied gently as she looked over at Amos and Otis who turned to walk away.

"You ain't gotta leave," I said to them, chuckling.

"We gonna go check on that water...see if it come to boil," Otis replied as they went into the house.

"Come here, baby, c'mon, look at me...now you listen to me, look at me, chin up," she said, working for my attention as she put her hand under my chin, gently nudging up to meet eyes.

"Yes ma'am," I replied softly, settling down as I began to cry.

"Gimme your hand, baby...put your hand over my heart, jus like I doin' to you," she instructed, softly gripping my hand, placing it over her heart. "You feel that?" she spoke with love, looking into my eyes.

I slowly nodded my head.

"That there, that, that's a blessing in itself, a *true miracle*...and it's jus the same when it don't beat no more. We can't go on forever, sweetheart, that ain't the purpose of all this...this life, this time, our time...but as long as we still got that beating inside us, long as grace keep givin' us time, she gonna be there, right there...*in every beat along the way,*" she explained with great care, not once taking her hand off my chest while she held my hand against hers.

My heart sank.

"Hope?" I questioned as tears ran down my cheeks.

"*Boy...was she sure fond 'uh you,*" she added, smiling gently as she wiped my cheek with her thumb.

"She gone?" I asked, fearful of the very words.

"She's gone, baby, our Sugar passed on," she spoke softly.

I broke down like never before; screaming, crying...I was so angry.

Ms. Violet wouldn't let go of me; she held me tight as we sat in the grass next to the open trunk of the car where the drum filled with snow sat still full, and she spoke loving tender words to me, for what seemed like forever.

That was nearly twenty years ago. I left that day with Otis, Amos and Lucky, after a long and very sad goodbye with Ms. Violet and Mr. Charlie. I always thought I would return for a visit but never did; it was just too hard knowing that Hope was gone.

Here I stand now, at the graves of Ms. Violet, Mr. Charlie, and my first best friend, little Miss Hope, all next to one another. Each of these lives shaped mine in ways that I'll never grow out of, and will forever hold dear to my heart. Even as I speak of my time with them or find myself making room in conversations where I can talk about Hope, or the sweet offerings from miracles, I ever so fondly refer to it all as, **Sugar**.

AUTHOR NOTE

Thank you to the film 'Stand by Me' for inspiring me at a very young age, and for helping me realize that the journey is just as important as the destination...and sometimes, even more so. But most of all, thank you for making me want to go on adventures and drink soda pop as I listen to old music.

It's Always Love.

For any additional work or to simply visit the world through his eyes, you can visit Kevin's website, where he often exposes the bond of hope which he so strongly believes we all share.

www.kevinsemeniuk.ca